INTERRAIL

INTERRAIL

Alessandro Gallenzi

ALMA BOOKS

For my family, who were right

How can you condemn a man who found himself equipped with a heart vigorous enough to love all the lovable women in the world?... By what unjust and bizarre whim would I restrict a heart such as mine within the narrow bourns of a single society?

Xavier de Maistre

DON GIOVANNI:

È tutto amore!
Chi a una sola è fedele
verso l'altre è crudele, io che in me sento
sì esteso sentimento,
vo' bene a tutte quante:
le donne poi che calcolar non sanno,
il mio buon natural chiamano inganno.

1

Rome, Bologna, Munich

THERE'S NOTHING TRUER and more sinister than what Pascal once wrote: that if Cleopatra's nose had been a quarter of an inch shorter, the entire face of the earth would have been changed. That Saturday morning, as Francesco was climbing off the train at Munich Central Station, one of the three old spinsters who are said to weave our destinies took her eyes off the spindle for a moment, and the thread she was holding in her hands got all tangled up. This kind of accident, though not uncommon in a man's life, can drive people down uncharted and unpredictable paths.

The day had promised to be beautiful. A ray of light had filtered through the blinds of Francesco's coach, jogging him awake. With somnolent eyes he had opened the doors of his compartment and peeked out into the corridor: through the windows, snapshots of the Alps were flickering by, bathed in the haze of sunrise. As he gazed out, he remembered his solitary departure from Stazione Termini, the girl from Berlin he had met and played chess with on the train to Bologna, and his spectral night tour of that city's deserted centre before boarding the 00.47 overnight *Espresso* to Munich. Then the image of his father giving farewell blessings, in a sauce-stained vest and unzipped shorts, strayed into his thoughts.

"If you wanna go on this Inter-Ray, then it's fine by me," the old man had said. "You've bought the ticket with your own money, so good luck. But then don't come knocking on this door for help if something goes wrong. Do you understand?" And to press the point, he had banged the door in his son's face.

Soon other passengers began to rouse themselves. Outside, as the sun ploughed across the sky, the fields revealed herds of sheep and cattle, with trees and little wooden chalets clinging to the mountainsides above, while inside people were waking up and shambling into the corridors to stretch their limbs or smoke their first cigarettes of the day. At last the wheels started to screech as the train pulled into the Hauptbahnhof. Passengers got out of their compartments dragging heavy suitcases, outsize cardboard boxes, surfboards and even in one case what looked like a ping-pong table. Francesco queued in the corridor with his small Invicta shoulder bag containing all he needed: a pair of jeans, spare shirts and underwear, a jumper, a map of Europe, a notepad, a pen and two books.

It was just at this point that the Fatal Sister lost her thread.

As he was putting his foot forward to climb out of the train, the woman behind him, impatient to get off, gave him an inadvertent push, and he missed the footboard and landed on the platform face first. For one long moment, all was dark. When he came to, a knot of curious onlookers had gathered around him. He sat up and then stood, signalling he was all right, though his nose was bleeding and he felt as if it was on fire, and there was blood in his mouth. As the passengers dispersed and flowed towards the exit, someone tapped him on the shoulder. Francesco turned and, through a cloud of cigarette smoke, saw a man of about forty, wearing a beige cotton suit and a loose white shirt unbuttoned at the top. He had a most extraordinary face, with a hooked nose of the Mediterranean variety, slanting eyes, a large mouth and a protruding chin.

"*Tutto a posto?*" he asked, taking another puff on his cigarette. "You all right?"

"*Sì.*"

"Take this," the stranger said, pulling a handkerchief out of his pocket.

"Cheers."

Francesco dabbed his nose and his inside lip, then looked at the red blotches of blood on his hands and on his T-shirt.

The man patted him on the shoulder and said: "You'll survive. Come on, let me get you a cappuccino and half a pint of blood."

They sat at a table of a coffee shop nearby. The man waved at the waitress and ordered cappuccinos, mineral water and croissants. Then he took a small silver case out of his breast pocket and offered Francesco a cigarette.

"Thanks," Francesco said, picking one and putting it in his mouth.

The stranger gave him a light from his own cigarette, then said, after taking a long drag: "So, what are you up to in Munich?"

"InterRailing."

"On your own?"

He shrugged. "A friend of mine – Leonardo – bailed out on me at the last minute. Says he's too busy, trying to write a novel. He decided to stay with his mummy."

"Ha! You been travelling long?"

"Not really. I left yesterday."

"Where from?"

"Rome."

"Rome? That's where I've just come from. Where are you staying?"

"Don't know. Some youth hostel, I guess."

"Well, if you want to get changed or take a nap, or even stay for the night, I've got a room booked in a place round the corner."

Francesco didn't say anything.

"Don't worry," the man added with a smile, stubbing out his cigarette with his foot, "I'm not suggesting we play naked Twister in the shower."

The waitress brought the order and the bill, which the stranger insisted on settling.

"You ever been to Munich?"

Francesco shook his head. "I've never been abroad, actually." He took a last puff and put out his cigarette in the ashtray. "Where are you from?"

"Me? I'm from Corsica. From Ajaccio. My name's Pierre, by the way, Pierre Cordier."

"I'm Francesco." And they shook hands.

Once they were out of the station, Francesco asked Pierre if he could recommend any places to visit.

"There's loads. I tell you what: if you give me half an hour to check in and freshen up a bit, we can mosey around Munich together for a while. How's that?"

"Sounds good."

It was too early to check in, so Pierre left his luggage with hotel reception and went back outside to where Francesco was waiting. They headed towards the city centre in an almost straight line, until they reached a square where a large crowd of people was milling about, gazing up at the tower of a sturdy neo-Gothic building. Pierre explained that three times a day – at eleven, twelve and five – the bells of the tower chimed the hours, accompanied by a carillon and clock with moving statuettes. Since it was only a few minutes to eleven, they decided to stay, and watched the carousel of dancing figures right up to the third cock-a-doodle-do of the gold-plated cockerel. Then they followed a noisy group of Italian tourists to a smaller square, which was even more packed. On all sides there were stalls with every kind of food, and people sitting on long wooden benches drinking from massive jugs. At the centre of the square there was a kind of maypole, decorated with the emblems and flags of Bavaria.

"Fancy a beer?" Francesco ventured, inspired by the joviality of the place.

"Sure. And some grub. That little restaurant over there looks all right."

Pierre chose an empty table and ordered drinks.

The beers were brought over. Francesco took a sip and asked, wiping froth from his lips with the back of his hand, "So what kind of job do you do?"

"What kind of job do I do? Well" – Pierre took some time over this – "you could say I'm a jack of all trades. But mostly I am a poet."

"A poet?"

"Yeah. I deal in finance. And money is a kind of poetry."

Francesco laughed.

"Although some people claim that finance is the supreme form of institutionalized theft," Pierre added, almost as an afterthought.

"Oh yeah? Why's that?"

"Why? Because they say the capital used to produce profits should belong to the exploited labourers. But then again, there are two kinds of people in the world: those who pull the cart and those who sit in it." He lit up and added: "It's money that makes the world go round and stops society from falling to pieces. It's always been like that – history began not with the taming of fire or the invention of the wheel, but when the first coin was minted." He took a longer drag of his cigarette and exhaled a large cloud of smoke, then emptied his glass. "You should read *Das Kapital* – it's every bit as entertaining as *La Gazzetta dello Sport*."

Food was ordered and delivered to the table, followed by another round of drinks. Once they'd eaten and drunk their beers, two more frothy jugs landed in front of them. The conversation took on a philosophical turn. Pierre began to talk about saints who had fled to the desert, hermits in the mountains, Diogenes and other ancient thinkers who renounced all social life in order to embrace poverty and personal freedom. He explained that all great men had despised money and the rules and constraints imposed by society, which he compared to a big chicken run.

"'Behold the fowls in the air,'" he continued in a deeper tone, with a slight slur, widening his eyes for effect, "'for they sow not, neither do they reap nor gather into barns – yet your heavenly

Father feedeth them.' You know who said that? Long hair, goatee beard, walked on water?…"

"So we should all flee to the desert?" asked Francesco, deadpan.

"I wish we could, but life's a bitch. Money can give you freedom, but it can make you a prisoner too."

When the bill arrived, Pierre again insisted on settling it. There was a problem, however: none of his credit cards seemed to be working, and he didn't have enough cash on him. Francesco offered to pay up with some marks he had exchanged before leaving, but Pierre said:

"No, I'll take this. You're my guest. Wait here."

Banks, however, were closed for the weekend, and the two cashpoints nearby wouldn't let him get any money out, so he returned to the bistro mumbling swear words to himself, and emptied his pockets onto the table with a mock-thespian gesture, producing just under eighteen marks in total. Francesco looked up at him and said:

"I think I'll have to help you shore up society today."

After another couple of beers in the square courtesy of Francesco, they worked their way back down Kaufingerstraße and stopped to see the Frauenkirche from the outside and, to get some cool air, went inside the Michaelskirche. Then they headed north and out of the city centre, towards the Englischer Garten.

"I used to go there when I was a horny young devil like you," Pierre said, "to do a bit of bird-watching near the nudists' area."

"The nudists' area?"

"There's some Teutons who like to sunbathe *au naturel*," Pierre said. "What's that face? You don't believe me? I'll take you there and show you an eyeful of apples and pears

– and bananas too, if that's what takes your fancy." He gave a wink and grinned. "I'll tell you a story. Once I went there in the morning with a German friend of mine. We were students then – full of pranks. We had binoculars and a little megaphone, one of those we used for our protest marches. There was this couple, about a hundred and twenty years old, who'd arrived before everyone else and stripped down to their bones – *uno spettacolo magnifico*. The man had a barrelful of guts drooping out, chicken legs and a tuft of hair clinging to his head. The woman was all droopy and wrinkly and jellylike: she looked like W.H. Auden's balls. Anyway, the man chooses a spot, spreads his towel out on the grass and puts down his picnic basket… The old girl picks up an apple from the basket and hands it to him. He's about to take a bite when my friend yells into the megaphone in German: 'It is heb-so-lute-ly *verboten* to eat in ze park!'" Pierre scratched his nose and suppressed a laugh. "Boy, you should have seen their faces. I nearly pissed myself, and the old man almost swallowed his dentures. The lady jumps up, looks around and starts flapping her arms about. Then my friend shouts again: 'It is heb-so-lute-ly *ver-bo-ten*…' – so they clear out without waiting to think twice…"

"Adam and Eve's Expulsion from the English Gardens," was Francesco's comment. He clapped his hands. "Shall we check out what ales they brew in the Earthly Paradise?"

After a long walk in the park, three more beers, a few ciga-rettes and a piss behind a tree near the Chinese Tower, they headed back towards the city centre.

"I need a shower," announced Pierre, definitely slurring now. Then he added, waving down a taxi: "Let's go back to the hotel."

"I have no money," Francesco pointed out.

"Jump in," Pierre said, and he opened the door.

"I have no money," Francesco whispered again, getting into the taxi. "How are we gonna pay?"

The driver, a Turkish man with silver-rimmed sunglasses, a golden tooth and formidable moustaches, asked where they were going.

"*Zoom Floock'afen, veea 'Otel Europa, beetteh*," Pierre said, closing the door behind.

"*Flughafen?* The airport?" thought Francesco, and darted an interrogative look at his companion, who reached out and gave his arm a furtive squeeze.

There was traffic, and the meter kept clicking away. Francesco broke out in a nervous sweat. Ten minutes later they stopped in front of a large hotel, not the one where Pierre had left his bags in the morning.

"*Un Moment, beetteh, veer 'ollen oonserr Ghebeck*," Pierre told the driver, as they got out of the taxi.

They entered the hotel, walked past a smiling receptionist and straight to the lifts, got to the first level underground, crossed to the far end of the car park to an emergency staircase and came out at the back of the building, onto a busy street.

"Now run," Pierre said. "Some taxi drivers know the trick. They've smartened up."

Not long afterwards they were laughing and drinking beer in Pierre's hotel room. They slept for around two hours, took showers, went outside again and spent the rest of the afternoon crawling from one *Biergarten* to the other, until the additional money Francesco had exchanged near the station at rip-off rates was reduced to a bunch of *Pfennig* coins.

"I've drunk too much," Francesco said, light-headed.

"You're right – I think we should eat something."

They sat at an alfresco Italian restaurant, went through a three-course meal, ordered champagne and the most elaborate dessert on the menu and did another runner. Breathless, they crouched down under a tree on the edge of the Theresienwiese and lit up a cigarette, bursting out into fits of giggles from time to time.

The sun was now setting, and their shoulders were hunched under the weight of the long, hot day. Francesco suggested they return to the hotel, and reminded Pierre he had hardly slept the night before.

"You what?" said Pierre. "We have a whole night ahead of us."

"And no money."

"I've got credit cards."

"Which don't work. How are we going to pay the hotel bill? We've drunk the minibar dry. I don't know if I've got enough cash."

"We don't need money. We are intelligent animals."

"Even intelligent animals need money."

"You're wrong." And he flicked the stub of his cigarette into the street.

Pierre's grey eyes were watching two parallel processions of ants moving in opposite directions by the kerb. It wasn't clear where they were coming from or where they were going, but at one point of the long line the activity was frenzied. The ants were bearing along a dead insect – a black beetle. Francesco admired the intensity, the determination, the spirit of sacrifice shown by those foraging little creatures, which for some reason reminded him of the Candle Race at Gubbio he had seen the previous year. The beetle seemed to be floating along on a black tide, and its movement was hardly perceptible. Pierre bent forward, stretched his arm and picked up the dead insect. After examining it for a short while, he wrapped it in a piece of paper and slipped it into his pocket.

"Intelligent animals don't pay: they only take or are given. Noodleheads pay."

"And you're either crazy or drunk," Francesco said with a smile. "Or both." He lay on the grass and looked at the clear sky, where the first stars were visible. Once more, the scruffy figure of his father tried to break into his thoughts, but he chased it away, along with other unpleasant memories of his life back at home. He had moved out of his parents' flat the year before, and although he had managed to get by without their help, life on his own had been tough. He had a university scholarship, but the textbooks for his language courses were expensive, and he had had to work in the evenings and on weekends, teaching English to the offspring of wealthy shop owners and small-time industrialists or, even worse, waiting tables and washing the grease off dishes in grubby local restaurants run by despotic managers. Now in two days he had spent almost half of the money he had saved for his journey, and though his head was spinning and his throat was burning, he was happy and free, and felt he could travel and conquer the world.

The night felt like it would last for ever, and the following day they woke up just before noon. They showered and went downstairs with their bags.

"Are you checking out, sir?" said the blonde girl at the reception, baring pink gums and equine teeth.

"Well, actually we have a big problem," Pierre said with an annoyed expression. "I'd like to speak to the manager of this establishment."

The girl lost her smile: in fact, it was as if all her teeth had fallen out.

"What is the problem, sir? Maybe you could talk to me?"

"I don't think so. I want to speak to the manager."

"Let me see if the assistant manager is in."

"Perhaps I didn't make myself clear," Pierre said in a dry tone, raising his voice. "This is not a matter that can be discussed with an assistant's assistant or an assistant or an assistant manager." The girl flushed red. She was alone at the reception desk, there were other people waiting to be served behind Pierre and Francesco, and the phone had started ringing.

"*Einen Moment, bitte,*" she said, and slipped out through a door that opened behind her. An urgent confabulation in German was heard, a few stifled shrieks and exclamations, followed by the rustling of papers, tapping of keyboards and interrogation of telephones. After a while, the receptionist re-emerged from the room with a taut face and, telling Pierre "the manager will be with you in a minute", she turned to attend to the other guests.

Several anxious moments passed. Francesco expected a Bavarian colossus to appear from behind the door, a giant of six foot five with a double chin and a long fluffy beard. Instead, out of the room came a sort of gnome – not one of those wicked little trolls you find in scary tales, but a kindly sprite with the most peaceable expression in the world – a tiny shrimp just about five foot tall, and as thin as a stick insect. He did have a beard, yes, but it was just a sparse goatee – and that was all there was to him.

Pierre took less than a second to size him up, and said: "You're the boss?"

The other did not seem put off by the curt tone or the stare of his interlocutor. "Yes, sir, what can I do for you?"

"This place is filthy, Mr Mansoor," continued Pierre, whose beady grey eyes had spotted the manager's name tag on his uniform.

"Filthy? I can't see any rubbish lying around," tried to joke the manager. He cleared his throat and added: "All the rooms are thoroughly cleaned and dusted on a daily basis."

"A-ha. When is the last time the hygiene inspector called in?"

The manager's right eyelid twitched twice.

"The hygiene inspector? Why?... I can check... I can check now, if you wish." He seized the telephone and dialled an internal number. There followed a brief conversation in German. "My colleague is just looking into this."

"You're telling me that you, the hotel manager, don't know when the hygiene inspector last came round? It's unheard of. Is this a four-star hotel or some cheap, run-down joint?"

These last remarks rattled the manager's self-control. It was his good luck that, just before a sharp reply could leave his lips, the telephone rang once more. On the manager's face reappeared the expression of a benevolent gnome.

"My colleague is just bringing the certificate downstairs, all right?" he said. "But you haven't told me what the problem is, sir..."

"The problem, Mr Mansoor," said Pierre through his teeth, nodding his head, "is that this morning, when we woke up, we discovered that we were not alone in our room."

"Not alone?"

"That's right. We had company."

At these words, the elderly American couple who were being served by the girl, and another small group of Japanese guests sitting in the foyer, pricked up their ears.

"I beg your pardon?" the manager stammered out.

"How would you feel if you were paying over two hundred marks a night for a room and found a cockroach crawling around in your bed, uh?" And, at that, he pulled from his pocket the insect he'd picked up off the street the night before and placed it on the counter. "Keep it and frame it: it belongs to your clean-and-dusted organization. *Oonkeziefer*. Vermin. *Capisce?*" He brought the index fingers of both his hands up to his temples and started to waggle them up and down, mimicking the antennae of a gigantic Kafkaesque insect.

There was pandemonium. The receptionist developed an immediate interest in the first guest register she could lay her hands on. The manager muttered an unintelligible curse, the American woman nudged her husband and gave him a meaningful glance, while the Japanese group began to cluck away to each other.

Meanwhile, a young man came out from the room behind the counter. To judge from his face, he was the manager's younger brother. He was the "colleague" who was supposed to bring the certificate of hygiene. However, in his haste he had carried with him an entire musty old box file that, when laid on the counter, gave off a stench of cellar.

"You sure there are no cockroaches in there too?" Pierre said with a smirk.

With all eyes trained on him, Mansoor riffled through the contents of the box file, but he couldn't even find an out-of-date certificate, only invoices, packing lists, receipts and other bumf of no relevance.

"I'm sorry," said Pierre after a while, "but we have a train to catch in half an hour. Will you agree that we should not pay for the room and receive some sort of compensation?"

"Of course... I'm awfully sorry," said the manager, who now seemed to have spied an easy way of slipping out of this embarrassment. "We'll take care of the bill. Actually, let me give you some complimentary vouchers, which you can use at one of our hotels in Paris or London."

"Thanks very much, Mr Mansoor..."

And a few moments later they swept out of the sliding doors of the hotel and rushed to the station.

Pierre was headed to Cologne, and there was a train leaving in less than ten minutes. They managed to get on just before the doors were closed.

Their journey was long but enjoyable. With his usual cool and what seemed to be a sort of sixth sense, Pierre disappeared into another compartment when the ticket inspector came along, re-emerging the instant the coast was clear.

"Only noodleheads pay in Germany," he commented, taking his seat again.

They kept re-enacting the scene in the hotel: the flabbergasted expression of the receptionist, the manager's face when he saw the dead beetle, the long swinging antennae – and Pierre was so good at taking off people's voices and mannerisms that Francesco couldn't stop laughing.

"So, what's your next destination?" asked Pierre when they had been travelling for more than an hour.

"I don't know. Just going north at the moment."

"Why don't you stay at my place for a night? My wife won't mind. We've got a small apartment for guests, and we are having a party tonight."

"If you're sure it's no bother…"

They connected at Mannheim, and at around five in the afternoon their train started to weave its way into Cologne station. They jumped on a tram, and after half an hour or so arrived at a splendid villa with a view onto the Rhine, surrounded by lawns and trees and with a paved driveway. At the end of it, there was a red convertible Maserati Biturbo. They were welcomed at the front gate by a Maremma sheepdog. After being fussed over by Pierre, the dog began sniffing at Francesco and licking his hands.

"He likes you," Pierre said. "Wait here, I'll go and get the keys for your apartment."

He came back soon after and escorted Francesco to an extension at the back of the villa.

"Make yourself at home. Porn movies are in the cabinet under the TV. Just try not to be messy, OK?"

"Ha, ha, ha."

"Look, I've got to go and help my wife Vanessa set up the room for tonight's private viewing at the gallery. She was expecting me there an hour ago. Can you come, say, around seven-thirty for eight? There'll be plenty of booze and muff. Here's the address." He scribbled a note on a scrap of paper. "And here's a map of Cologne. That's where we are, Rodenkirchen, and the gallery's around here." He made a small circle at the junction of two streets. "If you want to have a look at the cathedral first, you can just walk from there: it takes around twenty minutes. All right? See ya." He headed back to the driveway, with the dog leaping around him as he shouted, "Attaboy, Jester, attaboy!"

2

Cologne

FRANCESCO LOOKED ROUND: it was a lovely studio apartment – much bigger, in fact, than his own flat or the one where he had lived with his parents and his older sister Marcella until the previous year. There were maps and paintings hanging on the walls, including a red Che Guevara print which looked out of place, potted plants and statues, and shelves sagging with art books and exhibition catalogues. At the far end of the room there was an easel with a blank canvas on it. An illustrated volume was spread open on a low wooden table, next to a telephone. Francesco looked at the cover, which said *Paintings by Vanessa Schreiber, 1985–90*. In the inside flap, a photograph revealed the author as a thirty-something Valkyrian beauty, while a short biography described her as the leader of the "Oneiric" movement, a radical school of painting that proclaimed its allegiance to far-left political ideologies. She appeared to have exhibited in the most prestigious art galleries across the world, and two New York museums had acquired some of her works for their permanent collections. Buried under the book, there was a slim pamphlet in German entitled *Kunst und Revolution*, printed in 1983. This must have been Vanessa's Marxist contribution to the theory of art.

Francesco took another look at the paintings in the room, and realized that most of them were Vanessa's work. He couldn't say he liked them or was impressed by them. No doubt some connoisseurs regarded them as sophisticated pieces of abstract art – no doubt someone somewhere would have been prepared to pay a chunky sum to own one of them – but for him they were nothing more than a meaningless muddle. "The sort of toothpaste-and-shoe-polish job a kid can smear over an empty canvas in the dark," he thought, soon dismissing the formulation, which sounded too close to what his dirty-vested, opinionated father might say while picking his nose or scratching his arse.

After a quick shower he got dressed and went out. The evening air felt fresh, and a pleasant breeze was blowing. The sky was clear again, the river was motionless and the trees were full of songbirds – all in all, it was not too different from a *serata italiana*. Jester came bounding up to him as he made his way down the driveway and out of the main gate.

When Francesco arrived in front of the two huge stone towers of the Kölner Dom, his heart hummed with a strange feeling. He had never seen a Gothic cathedral before, and the size of that massive black structure overwhelmed his senses, which were more accustomed to Romanesque grandeur. He wandered for a while around the building, then took a seat on a low wall and watched wave after wave of people streaming by in every direction. A group of tourists stopped nearby, and their guide, a snub-nosed redhead with a German accent, shouted as she brandished a yellow flaglet at the cathedral:

"The foundation stone was laid in 1248, and the building took more than six hundred years to complete. Generations of masons and labourers have worked on it, among wars, plagues, fires and other catastrophes. This is not only a monument to man's religious fervour, but also to the ambition and tenaciousness of the human spirit. Now, if there's anyone who likes fancy cakes and chocolates, I'll show you a wonderful café down on that side."

As the group straggled away, Francesco caught the brief exchange of an Italian couple.

"Not bad, is it?" said the woman.

The man shrugged. "These churches all look the same to me."

Francesco went inside, roamed around the crowded aisles and sat down on a pew, trying to make out the bright figures on the stained-glass windows on either side of him. Just as his eyes were trying to measure the depth of the structure and the vertiginous height of the ceilings, a priest walked down the nave to announce that it would soon be closing time. He stepped out into the dimming daylight and made his way west, leaving the cathedral behind him.

Pierre's roughly inked circle on the map turned out to be two streets away from the correct spot, with the result that Francesco wandered off in the wrong direction for some time and when he arrived at the door of the art gallery proceedings were already under way.

His host was standing in the middle of the room, regaling the numerous attendees with a few introductory pleasantries in Italo-Franco-Deutsch. Francesco was unable to catch a single word, but the audience greeted his comments with laughter and applause. A short speech followed, this time in English, from the artist whose exhibition was being launched that day, a young Mexican sculptor called Philodemus. He explained how his art aimed at revolutionizing the world's "two-dimensional bourgeois perceptual schemes with the aid of three-dimensional, mechanical plastic works" – in other words, small toy theatres. One member of the audience, who looked like an old Italian immigrant, asked him if his work had in any way been influenced by the art of the *presepe napoletano*, the Neapolitan Nativity crib. For a few moments Philodemus was confused, until Pierre improvised a translation. The artist seemed rather put out by this insinuation, and pointed out, with a certain pique, that there were no influences to the "natural-born wellsprings of his imagination", and that if he had any influences, then these must be the very greatest of contemporary masters, such as Carlos María Gutiérrez y Gallardo or Luís María Alvarez y Petardo – names that neither Francesco, nor the immigrant, nor most of those present would have known – who epitomized the marriage of Mayan traditionalism and Spanish innovation, as Philodemus emphasized in a somewhat obscure elaboration.

Francesco looked on, bemused. Modern art wasn't his thing, and the creator of those mechanical thingummies, in his military combat suit, with his enormous, bull-like head that swayed this way and that, with his arms as long as those of a Pithecanthropus, seemed himself, under the spotlights of the gallery room, to be the main character in one of his movable toy theatres.

The presentation, to the relief of the audience, lasted no more than ten minutes, and then everyone got down to the real task of schmoozing, with the help of a glass of wine or champagne. Francesco was having a look at the work on display when the Mexican artist, mistaking his idle curiosity for sincere interest, came over to him and started a conversation in English.

"They're entirely made out of recyclable materials."

"Hopefully there won't be any need to recycle them."

The sculptor stared at Francesco for a moment in consternation – then he got the joke and smiled, revealing big white teeth, with black shreds of tobacco wedged between them. Whenever Philodemus spoke, he was in the habit of chewing on a quid of tobacco that he would draw from a little pouch he kept in the front pocket of his camouflage jacket.

"No, I didn't put it very well," he corrected himself. "What I meant was they're entirely made out of recycled materials."

"Mm. Interesting."

"You see, the idea is to establish a parallel between modern society, based on the recycling of old ideas and conventions, and these pop-up theatres in which the materials are plastic objects, nuts, bolts, toothpicks, newspapers… in short, all the detritus of contemporary civilization."

"Like in the Middle Ages, when they would build cities using the marble and bricks from ancient monuments," said a little old fellow behind him, before knocking back a glass of champagne in one great gulp.

"That's so right!" agreed Philodemus with enthusiasm, and the two continued to chat together. Philodemus launched into a detailed analysis of his works, ranging from their pre-Columbian undercurrents to their "intertextual" allusions

– yes, intertextual, since he had endeavoured to select the bits and pieces he used in the "printed" parts of his work with the greatest care, using only articles that denounced America's neo-imperialist policies of capitalism, globalization, etc. etc. Maybe some of these ideas were perfectly valid – thought Francesco – but when they were expressed by a young man of more or less his own age, with that great tangle of hair on his big square head… And after all – he said to himself – when you need so many explanations to prove that a work of art really is beautiful, that's always a good reason for starting to feel suspicious. As his empiricist father would say, fine words butter no parsnips. He remembered the great dark bulk of the cathedral, its towers and spires, that vast collective work of art that man had erected to glorify his yearnings for the divine… and his absent gaze wandered along Philodemus's little trinkets, in which the human figures had been assembled out of old knick-knacks and the trees were made out of pieces of chewed tobacco. At least, Francesco *hoped* it was chewed tobacco.

The evening continued back at Pierre's villa, where a select group of around a dozen people gathered for dinner. In the entrance hall, greeting the guests as they arrived, stood the celebrated Oneiric artist, Vanessa, in a revealing cyclamen-coloured dress in crisp contrast with her blond hair and gold jewellery.

After a round of introductions, they found themselves in a large living room, decorated with every shade of luxury that is possible to imagine, from the overly decorated objects that crowd the homes of people with pretensions to nobility to the inevitable Swarovski crystal ware, that unforgivable tribute to tackiness. And of course there was no lack of precious works of art from every period and style, infusing the room with the aura of a museum.

Around ten thirty, after an aperitif served by white-liveried waiters, the guests were requested to take their places at the dinner table. Francesco was sitting between an American sculptor and a professor of oriental languages; Pierre sat opposite him, with a couple of German painters, while Vanessa was at the far end of the table, next to Philodemus, who would not touch any of the dishes that were served as "he had no interest at all in food". The most extravagant artistic discussions buzzed around during the course of the evening, such as the proposition that "conceptual art is one of man's greatest conquests, as it frees the idea, which is perfect, from the form, which is the imperfect husk in which the idea is embodied" or that "death is a journey, and there is no art without death".

Francesco could not remember a time when he had yawned so much in his life, not because he found those aesthetic disquisitions trivial or uninteresting, but because he was dead tired and longed to go to bed at the first opportunity.

But the party dragged on until well after midnight. Vanessa did not say a word to Pierre for the whole evening: she seemed to be cross and distant, although from time to time she would favour Francesco with an occasional glance or smile.

Finally, in good Italian style, the after-dinner liqueurs were offered.

"So, what plans do you have for tomorrow?" Pierre asked Francesco, slipping into the chair of the Japanologist, who had exchanged seats with him.

"I was thinking of jumping on a train in the morning," Francesco replied in English, out of politeness to the other guests.

"Where to?" asked one of the German painters.

"Oh, Berlin, probably..."

"And then?" asked Pierre.

"Then I don't know... I've still got nearly a month left on my InterRail pass. I'd like to travel a bit around Germany, and then visit Amsterdam, London, Paris... we'll see, I have no definite plans."

"If you stop off in Paris," squeaked the only other woman present, a wizened old bony thing wearing a black widow's dress, "you must absolutely go and see the Père Lachaise cemetery. It's a lovely place."

"Sure..."

"Hey bud," continued Pierre sotto voce: his piratical eye was starting to gleam from the effects of the champagne and a big Havana cigar he'd been smoking, "if you're going to London, we should see each other... I'll be there in ten days' time for an auction at Christie's. We can arrange to meet up for a drink or something... And I've got those hotel gift vouchers the midget gave us... what was his name?..."

"Mansoor?"

"That's the one!" and he gave Francesco a friendly slap on the shoulders. He'd definitely been knocking back the bubbly.

"Sure, sure. Let's talk about it tomorrow... I'm dropping off now," Francesco said in a whisper, while Vanessa kept glancing at him in a strange way.

As soon as he got back to his room, Francesco threw off all his clothes and took a quick shower. It was almost two in the morning when he finally switched off the light and slipped beneath the sheets.

But sleep wouldn't come for a while. As he rubbed his eyes and massaged his nose, still painful after the bump it had taken the previous day, or rather two days ago, he started thinking about Pierre, this funny character who advocated a life without money while living in a luxury villa surrounded by all the comforts of bourgeois life. Then he thought about his unfulfilled sister, Marcella, with whom he had shared a room until the previous summer, his long-unemployed dad, his fretting mum, aged before her time – all content with their small-town world, all seemingly resigned to their fate since their very first day on earth.

He was half asleep when a sharp noise – the sound of footsteps on creaking floorboards – made him sit up in bed with a start.

"Who's there?" he said, first in Italian and then in English.

The only reply was a light being switched on behind a recess at the back of the room, which revealed an open door and a staircase communicating with the rest of the house.

"Hello?" he ventured, with a hint of fear in his voice. Then he thought it must be Pierre acting out some drunken prank, and was about to call out his name when a woman's voice said:

"Do you mind if I switch this other light on?" A dark shape was outlined against the faint glow from the open door. Before he could reply, the light had already come on. It was Vanessa, still wearing her cyclamen dress, which revealed her shapely body and the teasing lines of her underwear. Her eyes were red-rimmed, as if she had been crying, and her forehead was wrinkled by a slender furrow.

"I'm sorry to disturb you at this time of night," she said in a German accent made more noticeable by alcohol, coming over to Francesco's bed, "and for entering your room like this... but there's something important I need to talk to you about, and I was afraid I wouldn't have time to do it tomorrow morning before you left."

Francesco was tongue-tied, and with an imperceptible movement pulled the sheet up to cover his chest.

"I hear you are going to Amsterdam," Vanessa went on, "and I was wondering if you could do me a favour..."

"Uh-huh," said Francesco.

"It's just a small parcel... private documents... I cannot send it by courier: it must be delivered by hand to this address." There was a creaking noise from the staircase at the back of the room, and she turned round for a moment. "Can you do it for me? Would you mind? Here are the directions." And she gave Francesco a small piece of paper folded in two. There was a long pause, which the woman interpreted as a yes. "If you have any problems, you can give me a call on this number. Here's the parcel." After another pause, Vanessa added, smiling: "If you do this for me, I'll know how to show my gratitude." She caressed his cheek. Francesco felt his head flit around the room like a deflating balloon.

"Please don't say anything to Pierre, OK?" she whispered. "Be in touch. *Bon voyage*."

Then the lights went out one after another, and in the distance he heard the door being closed again and footsteps receding up the wooden staircase.

"What the hell..."

Francesco felt the parcel in the dark and weighed it in his hands. It was a kind of padded envelope, very light and presumably filled with papers. He switched the light on for a few moments, looked round for somewhere to put it and decided to chuck it in his shoulder bag. Back in bed, he wondered whether he should do what he had been asked to do, whether he should hide Vanessa's entreaty from Pierre and what, exactly, a beautiful woman like her meant when she said she'd "know how to show her gratitude". He began imagining the most improbable intrigues and adventures, and struggled for some time to get back to sleep.

The following day, at around half-past seven, he heard Jester yelping outside and a light tap on the front door, then Pierre's voice calling out:

"Francesco?"

"Give me a minute…"

He leapt out of bed, slipped some clothes on and went to the door. When he opened it, the morning brightness almost blinded him, and he was forced to shield his eyes with his hand.

"Did I just wake you up?" Pierre said, glancing into the room and taking a puff on his cigarette. "What's up, man? You didn't sleep well?"

"No, but we went to bed late," Francesco said, rubbing his eyes. "I'll catch up on some sleep later, on the train."

"You had a good time last night?"

"Yes, interesting people."

"Pity you didn't have a chance to talk to Vanessa," Pierre said with searching eyes.

"Yeah, well, she was sitting at the other end of the table…"

"Listen," Pierre continued, "what have you decided about London?"

"London? Sure, we can meet there if it's not a problem for you."

"Problem? What problem? We can have some fun, like we did in Munich. Turns out I'll be there on the twenty-first – a week tomorrow. I have to bring some stuff over, so I'm going by car. Here's the hotel address. I have booked under my name, Pierre Cordier. Let's meet up there at around three o'clock, OK?"

"OK."

"Do you want to go back to bed or come up and have some coffee?"

"Just give me five minutes and I'll be with you."

Vanessa didn't show up for breakfast, which was a relief for Francesco. Pierre joked that his wife needed to draw deep from her main source of artistic inspiration, and apologized that she had not come to say goodbye. Francesco, however, read something else into her absence.

As they went out onto the driveway, Pierre insisted on giving him a lift to the station, and Francesco was happy to accept, since he felt pretty achy and exhausted. But he soon regretted his decision, because Pierre was one of those speed merchants who will do 90 kph in a 50-kph zone, and who, once enthroned in the bucket seat of a sports car, are gripped by delusions of omnipotence. The result was that fifteen minutes later, after going through a red light and narrowly avoiding a collision, his car screeched to a halt in front of Cologne's Hauptbahnhof.

"There was no rush," Francesco managed to say once his feet had made contact again with the ground, "my train won't leave for at least another hour."

"Time and tide wait for no man... By the way, before I forget, have some cash, for yesterday's drinks." He pulled out two hundred-mark notes and offered them to Francesco.

"It's all right, don't worry."

"Don't be stupid – you need money more than I do. Intelligent people don't need money." He winked, then added: "Take it easy... see you next week in London, ciao!"

He slammed the door shut, and his car sped off, making such a din that everyone turned to watch as it roared by.

3

Berlin, Wittenberg

IT'S AN AGE-OLD TRUISM that "travelling alone is not the same as travelling in company". Francesco's five-hour journey from Cologne to Berlin seemed to last much longer than the time marked by the hands of his watch. After the excitement of the past three days, he was overcome by a feeling of restlessness and boredom. His thoughts could not stop going back to Pierre, Vanessa and the package she had given him, and flicked through his mind as fast as the German landscape outside the window.

He kept turning over the sealed package in his hands, holding it up against the light, shaking it gently to see if it would rattle, even sniffing at it, but he couldn't work out what was in it. Did it really contain documents? Or was he smuggling money? A small piece of art? Drugs? The only thing that was clear to him were the instructions for the delivery: on his arrival at Amsterdam Central Station, he was to take such and such a tram, get off at such and such a stop, then go straight on, turn left, etc. etc. In the best spy-story tradition, the directives were concise and to the point. But what about the caress that Vanessa had bestowed on him? And why didn't she want him to tell Pierre about the parcel? He began to think that he had been a fool to allow himself to get involved.

When Francesco got off the train, the heavy breath of sun-beaten asphalt enveloped him, and as he emerged from the station he was greeted by a pungent whiff of fried onions. He asked the man at the hot-dog stall, half in English and half in German, which way it was to the Brandenburg Gate or Alex-anderplatz. But the man didn't seem to understand and waved his arms around in reply, until Francesco realized that, *nein*, he couldn't get there on foot, he had to take the U-Bahn. He nodded, thanked the hot-dog seller and headed off munching a frankfurter.

Alexanderplatz turned out to be a disappointment. It took him less than fifteen minutes to get there, cast a quick look round and go away. At this time of day the square was deserted, and its emptiness made it even more ghastly. It seemed to be nothing but a large geometric space, lacking any architectonic touch informed by an aesthetic vision: it was the incarnation of functional architecture at its greyest. It must have been dreamt up – thought Francesco – by some Stalinist planning official during the sweltering heat of an afternoon such as this, between a cup of black tea and an unfiltered cigarette, with the drone of a clapped-out Soviet fan whirring in the background. "Thank God Communism left us the life-enhancing works of Bertolt Brecht as well as these horrible buildings," he said to himself.

The Brandenburg Gate was hardly more interesting. Yes, of course, it was older, and it still retained some majesty, with its dinky little bronze chariot and its bas-reliefs in Hellenistic style, but it was the product of calculated imperialist propaganda, imbued with the same pompous rhetoric as its Soviet-era successors. Francesco remembered the scenes shown on TV three years before: people partying and dancing in this square, youngsters singing the 'Ode to Joy' and some other ribald songs under the influence of the barrels of beer they'd been swilling down. They were hammering down the wall. They were making history. And what was left now of that wall – of the hatred, division and suffering it had caused? Fragments of rubble, neatly packaged into little transparent plastic bags, one mark each – one mark for a brightly coloured piece of history…

It was a quarter past two, and Francesco had already taken in the main sights of Berlin. What was he going to do now? Jump on a train and head off to another destination? Take a look at the Zoo? Then he remembered the German girl he had met on the train to Bologna a few days ago. She had told him to get in touch if he ever happened to be passing through Berlin. He rummaged round in his bag for his notepad. Elke. Elke Wassermann, Rheinsberger Straße, Berlin. Yes. Maybe they could go for a walk if she was free? Or perhaps she could tell him if there was something else worth visiting?

A deep, cavernous voice answered the phone after the first ring. Francesco was slightly taken aback, but managed to mumble a few words in German and asked to speak to Elke. After a few moments, she came to the phone. She was delighted to hear from him, and she'd have loved to go out for a walk, but was already tied up for the afternoon.

"Maybe we can go out for a pizza this evening," she said, "and play another game of chess?"

"That would be great."

"Let's meet at eight thirty at the Pizzeria Fortuna in Schöne-weider Straße. It's not far from where I live."

It took him a while to write down the address and directions to get there, but he was able to say bye before the last coin dropped and the line was cut off.

He strolled over to the nearby Pariser Platz, whistling... Even the former East Germany, with all its trucks, cranes, diggers, holes in the ground and building sites, had started to look more cheerful. Francesco glanced at his watch, and a stray literary reminiscence gave him an idea for how to while away the time until the evening.

He stopped a girl walking down the street. Could she tell him how to get to Wittenberg? She shook her blond hair: she couldn't speak a word of English.

"Wittenberg?" he repeated.

"*Ach ja, Lutherstadt Wittenberg?*"

He nodded. She smiled and wrote the word "Ostbahnhof" in his notebook, pointing towards the underground station. He waggled his fingers to ask if it was possible to get there on foot, and the girl shook her head and continued to smile at him.

"Everything is beautiful in this country," he thought. "I could fall in love with a lamp-post here."

He thanked her and ran to the nearest S-Bahn station, and managed to catch the ten-past-three train to Wittenberg.

That city of real and imaginary personages exercised a myste-rious fascination over him. With a feeling of awe, he sat beneath the oak where Luther had burnt the papal bull excommunicat-ing him. And with melancholy pleasure he wandered through the cobbled streets of the old town and imagined the haggard figure of Hamlet strolling along arm in arm with Guildenstern and Rosencrantz as they emerged from a local tavern – then saw the solitary, disenchanted and world-weary shadow of Doctor Faustus returning to his gloomy study.

What he liked most about Wittenberg was the almost total absence of tourists. He saw only two Americans, father and son, drifting around with knapsacks on their backs and huge cameras with which they were trying to immortalize a little bit of everything – the market square with its statues and pigeons, the churches, the houses, and the door on which the great Protestant reformer had nailed his ninety-five Theses. When they noticed Francesco behind them, they asked him if he knew who owned the "fortress".

"I can't work out if the castle actually belonged to King Luther," the father said.

"The sign's not in English," his curly-headed son added, "and the letters are kind of funny."

Francesco had a look at the sign in Gothic script, shook his head, shrugged and moved on. After another quick stroll through the town centre, he headed back to the station to catch the six-fifteen to Berlin.

The train was rattling along through the German country-side when it started to slow down and, as it approached a tiny station, its wheels screeched until it came to a complete halt. Five minutes passed, then ten. The train remained motionless on the rails. Francesco started to drum his fingers on his knees, darting nervous glances out of the window and exchanging inquisitive looks with the two elderly passengers sitting in his compartment. After another ten minutes, which seemed to drag on for ever, a ticket collector opened the door and growled something in German. The two old fellows got up with a querulous whine and started to gather up their luggage, from which Francesco concluded that they had been told to get off the train. He tried to ask what was happening, but neither of them could understand him.

Soon all the passengers were standing on the platform of a little station out in the middle of nowhere. Everyone seemed quite calm, as if nothing was wrong and the Space Shuttle would stop by and come to their rescue any second now. No one complained, no one got excited or started cursing and stamping their feet in a rage as happens in Italy when this kind of thing occurs – which is every day of the calendar year. People remained calm and continued to read their papers, looking up every so often with the same kind of indifference that herds of grazing cattle show for the outside world. Francesco felt like screaming.

Among the passengers he recognized the two Americans, and he went straight over to them. Apparently, if they had understood correctly, a goods train ahead of them had broken down, blocking the line in the direction of Berlin.

"A German train breaking down? Oh come *on*!"

"They say we'll be here for at least another hour," said the father, "until the track has been cleared."

Francesco glanced at his watch: no way would he be able to make his appointment with Elke. Perhaps he could give her a ring and at least let her know.

He went up to the small station house, looked around for a stationmaster, peered into a half-open little door and asked the man inside if there was a public phone booth around. Following his pointing finger, Francesco saw the tail of a long serpentine of people waiting to use the only telephone in the station. Glumly he went back to the two Americans, who were also starting to betray some impatience. They were due to take a plane to Los Angeles that night, and there was just no frigging way they were going to be stuck in that goddamn place and risk not getting to the airport on time.

"We need a taxi," said Francesco.

"Where are you going to rustle up a taxi round here?" said the father.

Francesco suggested that they move out onto the road and try to get a lift to the outskirts of Berlin. The Americans greeted the idea with enthusiasm, and wasted no time in sticking out their big ol' thumbs the minute they set foot on the tarmac of the roadway.

The first vehicle to stop was a lorry kitted out with chrome rims, spoilers and air horns. The driver was a massive Viking with studded armbands, a ponytail and silver jolly-roger earrings. Two large orange skull-and-crossbones stickers were displayed either side of a HIGHLY FLAMMABLE sign on the side of the tank trailer. Francesco exchanged a glance with the Americans, which said: "No time to be picky." They climbed up into the cab and squeezed themselves into the long seat next to the driver. Tim, the older American, had the bad idea of mentioning that they had a plane to catch – and the Viking responded by upping a gear and overtaking other vehicles in an erratic fashion along the narrow countryside roads, to the accompaniment of his horn's horrible honkings.

By the time they had reached one of Berlin's outermost underground stations, it was half-past eight. Francesco asked to be dropped off there and, after a few hurried words of farewell and thanks, he started to run as fast as his legs would carry him.

He ran and ran, he jumped from one train into another, he pawed the ground when he was forced to wait for a connection, he scrutinized, shaking with impatience, the map of Berlin that Tim had given him, calculating the minutes and seconds he'd need to reach his destination. Then he was off again, running up the escalators, down further flights of stairs, along a half-lit street, down another fully lit street, where people were strolling about in serene indifference – stumbling, slowing down and pausing for a moment to catch breath, wipe away the sweat and look at his watch… And finally, in a state of total exhaustion, he found himself in front of the neon sign of Pizzeria Fortuna. It was nearly ten o'clock.

The waiter gave him an apprehensive glance when he saw him enter with his sweat-drenched T-shirt, staring wildly all around, looking for Elke – who, of course, was not there. Francesco poured out in breathless Italian that he was supposed to have met a girl there at a half-past eight, but couldn't make it. The waiter called his boss, Nino, who told him that he had not seen any girl waiting by herself that evening – and that no one had left any messages.

"Forged'abow German girls," Nino added, *"so' tutte pazzariell'."*

He offered Francesco a slice of pizza and a beer to cool down, and the use of the waiters' shower upstairs. As a good *compatriota*, he tried to comfort him by telling him a few anecdotes and jokes about the "Teutonic totty", but Francesco's mind was elsewhere, and even if he smiled, he kept kicking himself inside for having missed his appointment with Elke.

When he came out of the pizzeria, he had no clue which way to go – right or left, north or south. He didn't even have anywhere to sleep, and it was too late now to go looking for a youth hostel. Then he had an idea – and he clung to it the way a shipwrecked sailor clings to a piece of flotsam: he would get to the nearest station and let himself be carried away out of Germany.

There was a train to Prague at a quarter to one, and a train to Lund, in Sweden, at a quarter past eleven – so he had just a few minutes to make up his mind. He would have liked to have gone to Prague, but the thought of having to spend another hour and a half in a waiting room, only to be faced with another five hours in the train, was not appealing. The journey to Lund was longer, and certainly no less tiring, but at least he could get onto the train straight away and, if he was lucky, snatch a few hours' rest.

The Lund train, however, was rather crowded. He wandered from one coach to the next, but there wasn't a single compartment in which he could have stretched his legs. Eventually, he found one that was occupied only by a couple of girls, but just before the train left, three more people turned up, so there was no room for him to lie down. He was in for a sleepless night.

4

Lund, Stockholm, Elsinore, Copenhagen

APART FROM THE TWO GIRLS, who seemed to be either friends or sisters, Francesco's travelling companions were a tall, blond young man, with pale hollow cheeks and a pageboy hairstyle, a woman who – to judge from the *Le Monde* spread across her knees and the Parisian simper imprinted on her lips – was French, and another young man, a stocky fellow, also blond, but red-faced and wearing a leather jacket two sizes too small for him, the kind of thing a charity shop couldn't give away. After they had been travelling for a few minutes, he was already producing sonorous snores, to the hilarity of the other passengers.

As often happens on such occasions, laughter acted as a catalyst to conversation, and they were soon chatting away about this and that. It turned out that the girls were indeed sisters: they were returning to Norway after a holiday in the Austrian Alps – a long journey behind them, and a longer one ahead. The young man with pageboy hair, Christer, was doing a PhD at the University of Lund, and had been to Berlin to visit a friend. Francesco introduced himself as a third-year student of English and Russian Literature at the University of Rome on an InterRail trip around Europe. The French lady – an attractive, elegant woman, with long dark hair, about thirty-five years old – didn't take part in the conversation and remained immersed in her *Le Monde*. Every so often she would look up from her paper, as if to intimate that she had no time for all that nattering.

At one point, the conversation took on a literary flavour. Someone was quoting a poem about Nature by a German Romantic poet when Francesco claimed that he liked the beauty created or imagined by man more than natural beauty, giving precedence to visiting cities, monuments, museums and art galleries rather than to communing with nature. Astrid, one of the two Norwegian sisters, maintained that the beauty of nature cannot be surpassed, and that man, in his works of art, can only aspire to imitate nature's complexity. Christer, on the other hand, agreed with Francesco that man's works represented a perfecting of what is found in nature, and therefore were the "highest expression of created being". Whereupon Francesco quoted, in support of this view, the Keatsian postulate that "a thing of beauty is a joy for ever".

"The usual railway-carriage generalizations," said Astrid, shaking her head.

An hour or so into their journey, the carriage lights were put out. Francesco drifted into a pleasant doze, interrupted only a couple of times by the German ticket collectors.

But they all suddenly woke up at around four thirty, when they hurtled past a fast train heading in the opposite direction, and the rush of air made the top of the window slam shut with a sharp bang. Even the young man with the leather jacket came to with a start and looked round, smiling bleary-eyed at the other passengers. He then turned to Francesco and addressed him in a language he couldn't recognize.

Francesco exchanged a perplexed glance with Christer and Astrid, who raised their eyebrows and smiled in amusement.

"Sorry, I don't understand," he said.

But the man carried on unabashed: he was winking and nodding all the time in the direction of the Frenchwoman sitting next to Francesco, extending his rotten-toothed smile to her.

"I'm sorry. *Non capisco. Nicht verstehen.*"

The other just carried on blabbering away, faster and faster. The Frenchwoman, meanwhile, decided she'd had enough and went to sit outside in the corridor. The man now started to show some impatience. He sat right next to Francesco, pulled from his pocket a piece of paper and a pen, and jotted down scrawled cursive letters, accompanied by a few little sketches to make his meaning clearer, then he went back to his seat and started to mutter to himself, clearly unhappy.

"*Govorit' po-russki?*" Francesco ventured, having sat his first Russian exam in February.

"*Moy drug!*" the man exclaimed. "*Ty govorish po-russki?*"

Now Francesco was *really* his friend. The man sat next to him again and pulled from his wallet a photograph of his girlfriend, Ewa, then a bottle of vodka from the breast pocket of his jacket, and however much Francesco demurred and tried to wave it away, he had to take a little sip – just one, come on – he couldn't refuse. Then all of a sudden the man turned serious and asked him, "*Pasport? U tebya yest pasport?*"

Francesco shook his head, again not understanding.

"*Yest u tebya pasport? U tebya pasport yest?*" the man repeated, and pulled from his jacket a whole packet of passports, which unfolded accordion-like in front of him. "*Bes problem, bes problem...*" he continued, putting his arm around Francesco's neck. "*U tebya dyengi yest, moy drug? Dyengi?*"

"*Dyengi?*" Francesco asked in bewilderment.

"*Dyengi... dyengi...*" he continued, pulling a wad of dollars from his wallet.

Christer explained that the young man was trying to sell him a passport to get into Sweden.

"I've got an Italian identity card."

"That's not enough," Christer said, "unless you are travelling with someone from Sweden who'll be having you as a guest."

"I didn't know that."

"Don't worry," Christer added, "I'm happy to warrant for you."

"*U tebya pasport yest? Pasport...*" the other was saying, giving him little nudges.

Francesco shook his head with vigour, but his friend continued to say, "*Bes problem, bes problem moy drug...*"

Just as it seemed that things could not get more farcical, the Frenchwoman came back, and Moy-drug relinquished his seat for her with a solemn bow and a salvo of smiles, nods and sly whispered comments in his unintelligible language – Bulgarian? Hungarian? – addressed not only to the Frenchwoman but also to the other passengers.

"*Ferme-la, espèce de voyou!*" yelled the Frenchwoman.

"*Nu ligger du illa till!*" Christer rejoined.

"*Det er for sent...*" said Astrid.

"*Che Babele!*" rounded up Francesco.

And they all burst out laughing. Moy-drug shook his head and continued to mumble something to himself for some time, then huddled up in his seat and relapsed into silence, soon falling asleep again.

At around half-past six, two border policemen came into their compartment and asked to see their papers. When Francesco showed his ID, the police asked him something in Swedish, and Christer confirmed that he was travelling with him and would stay in Sweden for just a few days. Then came Moy-drug's turn. It transpired that he was Polish. The policemen scrutinized his papers, then exchanged glances and asked him to go to the station with them for further checks. The young man, still rubbing the sleep from his eyes, tried to remonstrate in his language with a kind of muffled whimper, then turned to Francesco in Russian, seeking help.

"*Moy drug…*"

He was last seen getting off the train and being dragged away by police officers as he continued to protest and gesticulate, showing his passports and the photo of his girlfriend. A few minutes later, the train was rolling onto a ferry heading for Sweden.

During the crossing, Francesco had time to get to know Christer a little bit more. He was doing a PhD in philosophy and theology and, in his personal quest for the unattainable truth, he did not seem to disdain falling back on the Latin adage "*in vino veritas*" – or, perhaps more accurately, "*in spiritibus veritas*", since he was carrying in excess of five litres of whisky, vodka and suchlike rotgut in his rucksack.

"They're so much cheaper on the Continent," he explained. "Would it be OK if I give you two or three bottles before we reach customs?"

As a recompense for his bootlegging services, Christer invited Francesco to stay a few days at his place in Lund. Christer shared his flat with a Finnish student, Kimmo, a girl called Anne and her Irish friend Kyle, who would be leaving the following day.

When they got there, they had breakfast in the living room. Francesco had a look around and said: "This is nice. Must be very expensive."

"What do you mean?" Christer said, buttering some bread. "We don't pay anything. It's all subsidized by the State. We just have to do some work for elderly and disabled people from time to time."

"You are telling me that the Swedish government gives you a brand-new flat, fully furnished and with all mod cons, in return for a few hours of social work every now and then?"

"Not just us – most university students."

"That's fantastic," said Francesco.

"That's terrible," retorted Christer. "We live in a nanny state. Everything's served up ready-made for you on a silver plate, and you don't even have to worry about getting a job."

"Well," Francesco said, "in Italy there is nothing ready-made and no jobs, and all the silver plates and the cutlery have been stolen by the government."

"What are you talking about? Italy's a wonderful country."

"Italy's a place where anything is possible – if you are un-scrupulous enough."

"I am not sure which country is worse, then," said Christer.

"I wonder how the suicide rates compare," Francesco tried to joke.

He looked out of the window at the austere stone façade of Lunds Domkyrka in the distance and the oppressive leaden sky overhead. One thing you could not get in Sweden was good weather – and Francesco doubted whether the Swedish authorities, so efficient in every other respect, could do anything about that. Hence, no doubt – he reflected – the need for whisky and vodka, to help open a chink of alcoholic merriment in the all-enveloping greyness of life.

That evening Francesco followed Christer and his flatmates to a students' disco. Kyle was there too, and she sat next to Francesco and they had a drink or two while they watched the others dance.

"So you're going back to England tomorrow?" Francesco said.

"Yeah, I've got to do some work for my DPhil."

They talked about their studies, and because the music was very loud, they often had to speak in each other's ears and kept brushing their cheeks.

"I like the way Christer dances," Francesco said. "He looks like Nena singing '99 Red Balloons'."

Kyle burst out laughing – a full, hearty, Irish country girl's laughter.

"Seriously, look," Francesco continued, "either he's pooped himself or his arms are too long. I've never seen anyone so un-coordinated. I think he's coming unbolted."

"Oh, stop it!"

They had another drink and continued to chat for a while. Then Kyle suddenly ran her finger down Francesco's face and said:

"You're cute."

"You're more than cute." He paused to caress her auburn hair. "You're beautiful."

"Shall we go back to the flat? I want to give you a present before I go."

Ten minutes later they were undressing each other on the living-room floor. They lay down on the mattress on which Francesco was supposed to sleep and bundled themselves under the duvet. They were kissing each other and getting hot and bothered when the front door opened – and they froze. They heard some footsteps, then silence. Then the noise of someone opening the fridge and closing it.

"Must be Anne," Kyle whispered, "she's always been the party-pooper."

"Shh."

After a few moments, the living-room door opened a crack, revealing the tall shadow of Christer holding a bottle in his hand. Kyle took refuge under the duvet.

"Are you asleep, Francesco?"

After a long pause of deliberation, he answered: "No."

"I've brought some red wine."

There was another very long pause.

"I'm on antibiotics."

Kyle's muffled giggle could almost be heard. A long silence followed.

"Tomorrow's my twenty-seventh birthday. Will you give me a kiss?"

"Not today, thank you."

Kyle had to put a corner of the duvet in her mouth and bite hard to avoid bursting into laughter. The door closed, then opened again.

"Don't worry, I'm not going to seduce someone who doesn't want to be seduced," said Christer's shadow.

"OK. Goodnight."

And the door closed again. Kyle and Francesco remained under the duvet together a little longer, laughing under their breath, but love's spell had been broken, and a few minutes later Kyle got dressed and sneaked to her friend's room.

When Francesco woke up the following morning, he found out that Kyle had already left with Anne for the airport. There was a short note for him:

"Next time lucky? It was fun anyway. Let me know if you're coming to Oxford. My address and phone number on the back. Call me. – Kyle xxx."

Christer was having breakfast at the kitchen table, reading Heidegger's *Sein und Zeit* with a morose expression on his face.

"Sorry about last night," Francesco tried. "I had such a migraine, I had to go to bed early."

"Yeah, yeah," Christer said, without looking up.

"Well, happy birthday," Francesco said.

"Go to hell."

Kimmo entered in striped pants and sat opposite Christer at the table.

"Whassup?" he said.

As he brewed up a pot of coffee and ate some cereal, he told Francesco that he'd be leaving for Barcelona the following day for a friend's wedding.

"I'll stop over in Copenhagen and Amsterdam. I've got some friends there. We can travel together for a while."

"Sure."

That morning Francesco took a train to Stockholm – a four-hour journey which was made less unpleasant by the memory of the previous night with Kyle. Stockholm itself felt cold and austere to him. The same air of frigidity that pervaded Lund's cathedral seemed to be spread over that most northerly of the "Venices of the North". He wandered around the city's streets struggling to find something that would move or excite him, something characteristic or memorable: everything seemed linear, regular, quiet, clean – no asperity to snag his attention. When a sunbeam penetrated the clouds above, forming an oblong quadrangle of sunshine on the ground, he sat by the pedestal of the bronze statue of St George and the Dragon in Köpmantorget and ate his sandwich to the touch of a lukewarm breeze: that was the high point of his trip. Early in the afternoon, he was already on his way back to Lund.

As he walked up the stairs to Christer's flat, Francesco was steeling himself to weather another major sulk or renewed approaches from his host. But he shouldn't have worried, because Christer was in the merriest of moods and in good company. Stepping into the flat, Francesco saw him drunk and naked in the bathtub with a leather-thonged friend in an Alex DeLarge mask who was brandishing a bottle of Scotch and squirting shaving foam as they both chanted: "Happy birthday dear Christer... happy birthday to you!"

On the kitchen floor, inside an inflated condom, there was a message from Kimmo explaining that he'd be sleeping at some friends' place that night and asking Francesco to meet him at the station the following morning.

The next day Francesco woke at 6 a.m. and, having pinned a perfunctory thank-you note to Christer on the kitchen noticeboard, left for the station. After an early departure from Lund, Kimmo and Francesco stopped at Elsinore on the way to Copenhagen, in homage to the melancholy friend of Yorick. But Kronborg castle, too modern and too neat, and haunted with open-mouthed, audio-guided tourists rather than unavenged royal ghosts, didn't live up to Shakespeare's imagination. The church of St Olai in the old village, on the other hand, for all its stark mementoes of death and its bare look of a white-painted coffin, was a pleasant architectural surprise.

They reached Copenhagen just before noon. Kimmo's friend – an American fauve painter called Brian – lived in Freetown Christiania, the city's notorious commune. He shared a large detached house with another half-dozen Christianites, who included a Costa Rican pole-vault athlete, a local cannabis grower, a Moldovan theorbo player and a mother and daughter from Cologno Monzese. A long table was laid on the front lawn, and large portions of curry were dished out to the guests. The Moldovan girl did not eat a thing, but sat in a corner of the garden playing Baroque music on her weird, long-necked instrument, pulling the most atrocious notes and faces. She had long raven hair, dark eyes and wore a décolleté black dress. Her skeletal white frame looked lighter and thinner than the theorbo. Francesco was sitting near the Italian mother, and was curious to know how she had ended up in that place with her freckly fourteen-year-old daughter Mirella.

"We have come on holiday in May," the woman said in English, pushing up her glasses from the tip of her nose, "and we liked it, and so we said: 'You know what? *Ma vaffa a tutti quanti* – let's remain in Christiania.' Life is beautiful here, is free. No work, no traffic, no smog, no problems of money – we share everything. It's a kind of *falansterio*. We dig the earth, we cultivate yogurt, we grow potatoes, carrots, tomatoes, lettuce…"

"And practise all forms of sex in the fields," thought Francesco, noticing that the woman was trying to play an awkward game of footsie under the table.

"And what were you doing before moving to Copenhagen?" he asked, withdrawing his leg with a casual movement, so as not to offend her.

"I was a *supplente* – how do you say in English? – a…"

"A supply teacher."

"A supply teacher of Italian Literature. For twenty years. These days in Italy there's no hope of a *cattedra*, a *posto fisso* any more."

"A permanent position," Francesco explained to the people around.

"Yes. So we are all forced to become *zingari* – Gypsies – or exiles. That's the real motive we are here, I think. We're exiles."

By mid-afternoon everyone was drunk or high on weed, including Mirella and the Moldovan theorbo player, who at one point improvised a solitary *Totentanz*, before collapsing under a mulberry tree. Kimmo and Brian announced they were going for a "nap" inside the house, making it clear that they didn't want to be disturbed by anyone. The Italian mother asked Francesco if he fancied a nap too.

"Sorry, I never sleep in the afternoon," was his reply. "*Piacere d'averla incontrata.*"

And after leaving a note for Kimmo, he walked out onto the road and made for the station by the same way he had come in the morning.

5

Amsterdam

KIMMO AND FRANCESCO took the evening train to Hamburg, and then connected on the overnight service to Amsterdam. The coaches were dirty and crowded, and it was sweltering. During the seventeen-hour journey, they didn't manage to get much sleep, in part because of a young Belgian couple who seemed to be really going for it in the next-door compartment. It was with groggy eyes and achy legs that, around midday, they walked out of Amsterdam Centraal onto the sunny Stationsplein.

"I think I need a spliff," said Kimmo.

"I think I may need one too," said Francesco.

Kimmo had only three hours to spend before catching his next train, but he knew a place nearby where they could eat and get some first-class joints.

After they had polished off a large plateful of Surinamese food, drunk a few beers and smoked two long reefers, Kimmo insisted that Francesco also try the hashish-stuffed "space cake", one of the city's most celebrated specialities.

"Honestly, I think it would be too much for me," said Francesco.

"Come on, you've *got* to try it," Kimmo protested. "What's the point of coming to Amsterdam?"

So they ordered six slices, and Francesco took the first bite. Kimmo fixed him with an intent gaze and smiled as if to say: "Good, huh? You'll soon see how strong it is…" But ten minutes went by, then twenty, thirty, and not a single flying saucer came into view. Kimmo, on the other hand, seemed to be already on cloud nine or eleven.

"Hey, are you with me?" asked Francesco, giving him a shake.

"No, I'm not," the other replied, with a garish smile.

"Where are you, then?"

"Sitting on a winged gargoyle perched on the battlements of a castle."

"Good for you," Francesco said, laughing, "but you're supposed to be heading off to your friend's wedding in forty minutes. Come on, let's go back to the station."

After a few unsuccessful attempts, he managed to drag his companion off his seat and haul him out into the road. Pouring with sweat, he hoisted him across his shoulders to the tram stop, and travelled with him from there back to Amsterdam's Central Station. Once he'd seen Kimmo off on the right train and watched him wave goodbye through the window with a grinning face, he went back outside and drew a deep breath. He didn't want to admit it to himself, but he was feeling a bit funny – sort of hollow-headed. He took another long breath and decided to walk around and see if he could shake off his daze.

He took out the piece of paper Vanessa had given him, and the Amsterdam map he had bought at the station, and tried to locate the address where he was meant to deliver the parcel. It looked as if the place was more or less within walking distance, so he thought he'd get his errand out of the way at once. He made straight for the central square, the Dam, stopping to take a quick glance at the tourist sights, and then, leaving the Nieuwe Kerk behind him, he reached Raadhuisstraat and turned right.

He started to skip along like a quail – his feet seemed to move of their own volition. He had no idea what had come over him, but he felt happy, he felt liberated. He crossed the first canal, then a second, then a third and a fourth. Following the map, he passed the Westerkerk on his right-hand side, then turned right, then left, and then carried straight on for a long way, crossing more canals and rows of grey houses.

His legs were getting lighter and lighter, as if he were walking on cotton wool, and his face felt numb, almost anaesthetized. And then he was making his way over another little waterway and past a small park, before turning into a broad avenue, and then another, crossed by tree-lined, brightly lit streets, where dark-skinned boys were playing football, or floating through the air like so many little black angels.

After that, it was easy: he simply needed to show his piece of paper to an old hag who was squatting on the ground under a station bridge. Not the first road – she said – nor the second, but the third on the left. If not the third, then the fourth. He lit a match, and the witch was reduced to ashes in a single burst of flame. He started to laugh to himself: how easy it was. And to think he'd been worrying about this!

After a few minutes, he was standing in front of the building indicated in Vanessa's instructions. It was a tall red-brick construction with grey metal balconies looking over a little canal. He made his way to the main entrance across a small playground, where empty swings were rocking back and forth and newspaper sheets fluttered about. He rang the bell, and a raucous caterwauling came in reply. The doorway opened its maw, and he got into the lift. Up he rose – up, up, like a repressed hiccup in the steel gullet of the building – until he reached the fifth floor, the fiftieth, the five hundredth... But then the lift started to go down again, and it just wouldn't stop, it kept going down, even when he pressed the alarm button. Then its doors burst open, and he began to run. He wasn't alone: eyes were following him. His legs were still as light as feathers, and he took great floating strides through the air, defying the laws of gravity. He ran down long corridors, all identical, all deserted, riddled with green doors on which myopic peepholes opened. A thousand little jingles kept ringing round and round in his head to the accompaniment of his heart's tom-tom drumming in his wrists, his shins, his temples. He closed his eyes and continued to run, weightless, ethereal. And all of a sudden there was a great blaze, a wall of light into which his soul seemed to crash. Then he heard someone dashing down the stairs. Then darkness, then oblivion.

When he woke up, Francesco was lying on a bed in the white ward of a hospital. Seeing a wavering shape moving around the room, he tried to speak, but his voice was too thick and slurred to articulate even basic sounds. The shadowy figure hovered over him for a few moments, then its outline resolved to reveal a male nurse with gingery hair, holding a syringe. He smiled as he rolled up Francesco's sleeve. Francesco tried to sit up, but it was no use: it was as if he'd been put into a straitjacket and tied to the bed. And then he felt an incredible weight on his head. A needle pricked his arm, and he began to relax, though without regaining his sense of hearing or speech.

Perhaps two hours went by. The nurse kept going out and coming back into the room, glancing at him from time to time with the kindly expression of a priest wishing to comfort a dying man. But Francesco knew he wasn't dying: he could feel his energy coming back, the sounds becoming audible again and taking shape in his throat.

"Where am I?" he managed to say at last.

"In a hospital," the nurse replied.

"What am I doing here?"

"You're being kept under observation," the nurse explained. "They think you might have a concussion, and we are waiting for the doctor to examine the X-rays. "

"How long have I been here?"

"Since yesterday afternoon. Someone found you unconscious in a building in Slotermeer, rang the ambulance and—"

"Do you know where my bag is?" Francesco interrupted him, with a hint of panic in his voice.

"Which bag?"

It was just as Francesco feared: his shoulder bag, and Vanessa's package with it – as well as his notepad, clothes and wallet – had disappeared. Someone must have taken it. What had happened? Had he fallen awkwardly on the floor? Banged his head against a wall? Had he been hit? He couldn't remember. He reached for his trousers, which had been folded on a chair next to his bed, and searched inside the pockets. To his relief he found his InterRail pass and ID card in the back pockets, and in the front ones some of the money Pierre had given him the other day, which he had exchanged on his arrival in Amsterdam. He also found Kyle's note, with her contact details on the other side.

When the doctor – a pug-faced fellow with an olive complexion and an expression imbued with a sincere disgust for humanity – finally arrived, he cast a grudging look at the X-rays, then started to probe and prod Francesco's head as if he were checking a fig's ripeness. Every time the doctor's fingers pressed on it, a moan escaped from Francesco's lips, and at every moan he said something to the nurse, who was fiddling with another syringe.

"Ouch!" Francesco shouted when the doctor tapped on a spot above his right ear.

"It hurts, doesn't it?" The doctor went on tapping.

"Everything all right?" Francesco asked at last, impatient.

"Yes, I'm fine, thank you," said the doctor.

"I meant with my head."

"I know you meant with your head," the doctor rasped in a humourless tone, staring at him.

"Well, then?"

"Well then you tell *me* what goes on inside your cranium, young man. Have you been taking drugs – cannabis? Riding the world of illusions? That's what the blood tests suggest."

Despite the reprimand, the doctor's verdict was positive, and Francesco got off with a tight and rather conspicuous bandage around his forehead and temples. He remained in hospital under close watch, and spent the rest of the day and the following night in long, fuzzy spells of sleep, where he dreamt of singing with a ball in his mouth the size of a football pitch, of Vanessa frowning at him with a mischievous smile, of an interminable race to reach the top of a steep hill of glass shards, of the old black widow telling him he must visit Père Lachaise... Pièrre... Lachesis...

Early the next morning, Francesco was discharged from hospital. It was Sunday, and the streets were suffused with an atmosphere of lethargy and indolence. He consulted a new map of Amsterdam he had picked up from a hotel and began to walk towards the city centre. Soon the houses started to turn tall and narrow, the façades richer and forward-leaning, the gables more elaborate and snouted with hoist beams.

Francesco spent the morning at the Rijksmuseum, attending to the paintings with glazed eyes and a queasy feeling. In the afternoon, after grabbing a small sandwich, he meandered along the sunlit canals, wondering whether he should continue on his journey or return home, and whether he should try to get in touch with Vanessa and let her know about the parcel. He was heading towards the station to check departure times when, on an impulse, he decided to retrace his steps to Slotermeer.

The small playground in front of the red-brick building had taken on the reassuring appearance of solid reality: the swings were motionless, as were the leaves on the trees, and in the canal a few moorhens could be seen paddling by. Francesco followed them as they disappeared round the back of the building, and spotted a reddish mass next to the surface of the water – a kind of tattered old book, all soaked through. He dashed along the path adjoining the canal and bent down to fish up the object. But alas, it wasn't his notebook: it was just a filthy, sopping cotton sweater.

He had a look round and shrugged, kicking a stone into the water.

Dispirited, he returned to the main entrance of the building. He studied the entry-phone panel, but could not recall which buzzer he had pressed. He tried to remember the recipient's name or the flat number in Vanessa's instructions, but they also seemed to have been erased from his memory. Just as he was about to turn around and walk away, he noticed that the door was ajar, so he let himself in.

Inside, there were no signs of life. The doors were all alike, painted in green, with no name on them or on the wall. Francesco ventured down the maze-like corridors of the building, from one side to the other on each of the seven floors, desperate to find a clue or remember a detail of his previous visit. On his way back out, he inspected the second floor again. Perhaps it was autosuggestion, but there was a crack in the landing's wall that he thought he had seen before, and a smell that reminded him of the moments before he had lost consciousness. He decided to knock at the nearest door. When no reply came, he knocked again, louder.

This time a door opened, but it was the next one down the corridor on his left. A man peered out and said something in Dutch. Francesco shook his head, and the man added in English:

"It's vacant."

"Sorry?"

"No one lives there. It's been empty for some time."

"Oh."

"Can I help you?" The man was now standing in the corridor, with a half-opened book in his hand. His resemblance to Van Gogh was extraordinary – a real incarnation: the only things missing were the fur-lined cap, the pipe and the white bandage around his head, which Francesco could have lent him for effect.

"I wonder if you can," said Francesco, and walked over to him.

He told him about the mysterious accident on Friday, the disappearance of his bag and of a parcel he was supposed to deliver in the building, the fact that he had been knocked unconscious and left almost for dead until someone had rung an ambulance. The man listened in silence, then said:

"I'm sorry, I was working on Friday. Perhaps the caretaker knows something."

"Where does she live?"

"It's a he. His flat's on the lower ground floor, on your left as you go downstairs from the entrance."

"Thanks a lot."

"And oh" – the man lowered his voice – "don't mind his ways – he's a bit funny."

"Is he?" said Francesco.

"He's English – maybe Irish." He nodded. "They call him Mr Mephisto."

"Mr Mephisto?"

The man tilted his head and gave another ambiguous nod, then added: "Let me know if I can be of any help."

Francesco descended the stairs and found the caretaker's door. At his first timid knock, there was mayhem on the other side of the wall: a hubbub of barking dogs, interrupted only by short, troglodytic growls. The door opened: a thin, bony man of about fifty, with a beard and long, greasy hair, appeared in the crack, while a dozen dogs continued to bay, yelp and howl, trying to scratch their way out of the flat, from which emerged a pungent canine smell.

"Sorry to disturb you," said Francesco, taking an involuntary half-step back.

"What do you want?" was Mephisto's curt reply.

Francesco explained again in a few words, pointing to his bandage as he did so, about the accident of the other day.

"Yes, I've heard it from the postman yesterday morning. Come on in," Mephisto said, and opened the door, withdrawing into another room, while the dogs scattered around the flat in silence, wagging their tails.

Francesco followed him in and closed the door behind him. Mephisto was waiting for him in a small sitting room, decorated with crimson wallpaper and ghoulish prints. In one corner, on a small sideboard, lay some big round white stones. The bestial stench in this room was even stronger. Dog hair lay everywhere.

"Sit down," he said, as a mongrel sniffed the cuffs of Francesco's trousers. "Where are you from?"

"I'm from Italy."

"*Ittaliano? Oh, amicco mio! Buongionno, como estai?*"

"*Bene, grazie.* I'm all right."

"You don't look all right to me," Mephisto corrected him with a smirk. "Cognac, *vino*, whisky?" He poured a glass of reddish liquid and put it down in front of Francesco, who realized, through the corner of his eye, that what he'd taken for stones were in fact human skulls. He knocked back the liquor in one gulp, and it was so strong that he soon began to cough and splutter.

"Good stuff, huh? *Molta buona*," Mephisto said. "Oak-barrel-aged."

"Yeah…" Francesco noticed a baby Jesus hanging on the wall behind him. The bleeding heart was pierced by a tiny dagger.

"So, do you want to report this to the police?" Mephisto asked.

"Report it to the police? You mean the incident? Well, no, it's a bit complicated…"

"What is complicated?".

"Well, you see, a German lady had given me a parcel to deliver to someone in this building, and I've lost it… or someone's taken it."

"Oh right, an international intrigue… And what was in the parcel?"

"I don't know."

"You don't know. Mmm… Have another drop. *Brindiammo*." Mephisto poured him a second glass of whisky.

"I was hoping you'd found the parcel – or my bag, which has also disappeared."

"I've found nothing."

"Nothing."

"No."

"OK."

Francesco drank up the second glass, and this time he felt the alcohol go down his throat like a streak of lava, stirring up an incandescent vortex in the pit of his stomach. When he recovered from another coughing fit, he asked:

"Do you know who might have called the ambulance?"

"I've no idea. I have enough to worry about looking after this place." Mephisto poured himself half a tumbler of whisky, and knocked it back as if it were peach tea. "I'll tell you what you could do, though."

"What?"

"You could ask the building's managing agents to check the CCTV records for Friday." He removed the bookmark from a well-thumbed edition of *Lust for Blood* lying on the floor, and handed it over to Francesco. "Here's their card, if you want to get in touch. They're in the old city."

"Sure. I'll go and see them tomorrow morning. Something may turn up."

"I'll tell them you're going. Good luck. *In bocca a luppo!*"

"*Grazie mille.*"

Francesco returned to the second floor and knocked on the door of the man he had met before.

"Hello again," he said when the door opened. "Would it be all right if I made a quick phone call?"

The man looked at him for a few seconds.

"I'll pay for it," Francesco added.

"No problem. Come in."

Francesco followed him inside, into the living room. It was a nice flat with a view over the canal and large picture windows. Other than a few cardboard boxes huddled in the corners and a small table with two chairs, there was no hint of furniture. The place seemed brand-new.

He looked up international enquiries in the phone book and asked for Vanessa's number, but it wasn't listed. Then he called his family, but after three rings he decided to hang up.

"No answer," he said.

"You can try again in a few minutes, if you want," the man offered. "Can I get you a drink? Tea?"

"That would be great, thank you."

They sat at the small table in the kitchen area at the back of the living room and drank green tea.

"Have you just moved in?" asked Francesco, pointing at a stack of cartons behind him.

"Oh, no. I've been here for over three years. I've just never got round to unpacking my stuff."

The man explained that he was hoping to move out to the country very soon. He hated the daily commute to work, and he loathed cars and the city's chaos and pollution. Nature and quiet was what he yearned for, and despite being a scientist by training and an urban engineer by profession, his real passions were literature and art. That prompted Francesco to ask who his favourite authors were, and when the man mentioned Dante, Goethe and Michelangelo, the conversation blossomed. One pot of tea followed another, and only when dusk began to fall outside did Francesco clear his throat and announce: "I think I should be going."

"If you're not in a rush, we can get something to eat first," the man offered. "What do you think? We could go out for a pizza. Otherwise I can phone for a home delivery."

"I can bake some pizza, if you like."

"You can bake pizza?"

"Of course. Every Italian can – don't be fooled by my Indian turban."

The ingredients they managed to dredge up at the local supermarket weren't of the best: the flour wasn't the right sort, the dried yeast smelt of rotten cabbage – and, as for the mozzarella, it looked more like ancient Play-Doh than anything else. All the same, the final result, a pizza margherita topped with mushrooms, yellow peppers and courgette – named "Pizza Baldovino" in honour of Francesco's host Boudewyn – was deemed a great success.

"So what brought you here?" Boudewyn asked, as he was working his way through the crusts.

"I'm InterRailing."

"I mean, what brought you to this place?"

"Oh." Francesco took a sip from his glass of beer. "I told you before: I was meant to deliver a parcel to someone in this building, but it got stolen with my bag and I don't remember who it was for."

"I see," said Boudewyn with a thoughtful nod. "So what are you going to do about the parcel? Any luck with Mephisto?"

Francesco told him that he had drawn an almost complete blank, but that there was a small chance that the incident had been recorded on CCTV. However, since he didn't have enough money for a hotel, he might not be able to go to the managing agents' office in the morning, but would have to get on an overnight train, possibly homebound.

"Well, you can stay here for the night, if you wish," Boudewyn said. "I've got plenty of room, as you can see. I can give you my sleeping bag."

"You sure? That's very nice of you."

After a few more beers and a glass of whisky, Boudewyn ventured to read out some poems of his own making and translate a sonnet by Rilke, something about a headless torso – a fitting description of how Francesco was feeling that evening. By the time Boudewyn capped off his reading with the startling admonition "You must change your life", it was nearly eleven, and despite Francesco's politeness and his high regard for poetry, he felt it was time to ask his Dutch host whether it was OK to go to bed now. When the light went off, he was hoping that the night would bring him some quiet, but exhaustion and anxiety acted like a double espresso on his mind, and he had to lie there for a very long time trying to keep at bay his hazy memories of the day before he could drift off to sleep.

Towards dawn, he woke up goaded by a thought that must have flickered through his mind during his sleep. He jack-knifed out of the sleeping bag and whispered to himself: "The postman!" He took off his bandage and lay down again. Why didn't he think about it before? Mephisto had mentioned that he had heard about the incident from the postman the previous morning. Maybe the postman knew something. Perhaps he'd seen someone…

Not long afterwards, Boudewyn tiptoed into the living room and walked to the kitchen area, opened the fridge, poured some cold milk, cornflakes and oatmeal into a bowl, mixed muesli and marmalade together in a yogurt pot, spread butter and jam on a slice of toast and started to eat. Francesco waved his arm to show he was awake, and Boudewyn invited him over to the table. Francesco told him his idea of talking to the postman, and Boudewyn was only too happy to help.

"I'll call my office and tell them I'll be a bit late," he said.

Just before eight, they met the postman at the entrance of the building. Boudewyn introduced himself and asked him something in Dutch. The postman put down his bag and launched into a solo piece of sibilants and fricatives, a kind of prolonged "chshkhzhfhxh", at the end of which Francesco turned to his friend and demanded, "What's he saying?"

"He says he's from Friesland too. There aren't many van der Zouws in our part of the world – he thinks he knows my father by sight."

Francesco grinned and jabbed his elbow into Boudewyn's arm. "Ask him about the other day, if he saw anything."

The spluttering and cracklings of a badly tuned radio started up again. The postman pointed to the apartment block and flung out his arms in a gesture that embraced the whole district.

"What's he saying?" Francesco asked, the moment they paused for breath.

"He says that he's been working round here for over twenty years, and when he started it was still open country: there used to be a grove of trees where the apartment block is, until only a few years ago."

Francesco tilted his head and glanced up at his friend with mock anger. Boudewyn smiled in return and launched into further questioning. After a few more exchanges, he told Francesco that the postman had learnt about the incident from someone on the third floor, who had seen the ambulance arrive. He had not heard of any parcel or rucksack that had been found. After waving goodbye, the postman shouldered his bag and continued his round inside the building.

"Well, bad luck," Boudewyn said.

"Never mind. I can still try with the managing agents, even if it's a long shot."

Before he left for work, Boudewyn wrote down his office number, in case his friend had any problems. Francesco thanked him once more for his help and hospitality, and gave him his own contact details.

"You must come and see me in Rome."

"You bet."

On his arrival at the offices of Delta Groep B.V., the managing agents, a balding young man wearing a dapper suit and thick glasses asked him to follow him up to the next floor. Here, another couple of similarly dressed clerks were waiting for him.

"Mr Sullivan called," one of them said.

"Ah, Mephisto," Francesco thought.

They made him fill in a few forms in Dutch and English before taking him into a meeting room, where another bureaucratic figure loomed, large of frame and managerial of stature, behind a paper-free desk. A small television set was standing in the corner. Francesco sat down.

"Mr Mirabelli," the bureaucrat said, "my colleagues have reported that there has been an incident in which you were involved in one of our properties in Slotermeer last Friday. Is that correct?"

Francesco cleared his throat. "Basically, yes."

"Very well."

Just then, the bespectacled man appeared again with two videotapes and handed them with a solemn gesture to one of the clerks who had escorted Francesco there, who in turn passed them on to the bureaucrat, who fed the first tape into the VCR connected to the television set and drew the blinds behind him to darken the room.

"There's only one surveillance camera inside the building," said the bureaucrat. "It's by the main entrance. These tapes cover the whole of Friday afternoon."

The tape was fast-forwarded to the moment when Francesco entered the building, then it continued at normal speed. Francesco was seen getting into the lift and disappearing behind its closed doors. A few tense minutes followed, in which nothing happened. Then a bulky figure, surmounted by a huge square head, appeared on screen running down the last flight of stairs towards the exit. He didn't seem to have Francesco's parcel or bag with him. The bureaucrat stopped the tape and rewound it to show a still of the man's face.

"Do you know this individual?" the bureaucrat asked.

Francesco leant forward to have a better look at the quivering black-and-white image, then shook his head and said no.

The bureaucrat pressed play again until the mysterious man moved outside the camera's field of view. A few moments later a second person – a woman – appeared coming down the stairs, but only her legs and part of her waist became visible. The woman stopped a few steps from the landing, then retreated up the stairs and vanished. They examined the rest of the tape, until the paramedics arrived and took Francesco out on a stretcher.

"Would you like us to report this incident to the police, Mr Mirabelli?" the bureaucrat asked, opening the blinds.

"No, thanks."

The bureaucrat exchanged a significant look with his colleagues, then informed Francesco that, should he change his mind, the tapes would be kept for about six weeks before being recycled.

"I don't think it's worth the trouble," Francesco said. "Honestly."

"Very well," the bureaucrat said, while the bespectacled man stared at Francesco in perplexity, perhaps imagining God knows what spy caper or drug-trafficking plot behind the smokescreen of his reticence. Since it was obvious that at Delta Groep they didn't have time for hassles of this kind, Francesco soon found himself, without any further questioning, outside the bureaucrat's office, being ushered gently but firmly towards the exit.

"Mr Mirabelli, this is your invoice," said the man with the glasses, handing him an envelope.

"Thank you so much."

"That'll be thirty-five guilders in total."

Francesco came out of the building in a painful daze. He walked along the busy streets of Amsterdam staring ahead of him, not really knowing where he was going. He followed the curves of a large canal, took a little bridge to the left and a lane to the right. He continued to walk for a long time and ended up in the flower market, but carried on without thinking, and after a few minutes found himself back in the Dam, the central square. When he got there, he went straight to the station. He could have left for Milan in the early afternoon, but he got instead onto the first train for Brussels, then headed towards Ostend, and from there embarked on the night ferry for England.

6

London

THE FERRY THAT WAS TO TAKE Francesco across the
Channel was packed: there wasn't even a place to sit, let alone
lie down and have a nap for a couple of hours. Wherever he
went, he could not escape the small TV screens pumping out
British sitcoms and episodes of Mr Bean. A fat woman next to
him was chuckling like a turkey, and next to her a podgy little
boy kept fidgeting and wriggling and hopping and skipping
and whimpering and whining.

In the end Francesco did manage to get off to sleep, huddled
on the ground with a bundle of plastic bags under his head and
newspaper sheets covering his eyes. He dreamt of an old man
staring at him in silence, grinning a toothless smile as if to say
something, now and then darting a probing glance towards
Francesco's trouser pockets.

"Sir," the old man mumbled in the dream, pointing a stubby
peasant finger at him, "de wally..."

"Sorry?" Francesco replied, looking around.

The man screwed up his face into a delta of creases and smiles, nodding all the time. "De wally," he repeated, still pointing at Francesco's trousers and jutting his chin in that direction.

Francesco lowered his gaze, and seeing the gaping, toothless mouth of his empty wallet he woke up.

It was nearly daytime, and the break of dawn had driven away both the fat woman and the boy. The sea was a sheet of steel under a smoke-grey sky, and the English coastline seemed suspended in mist. A few drunken seagulls criss-crossed the view, taking sudden plunges into the water.

There were long queues first to get off the boat and then to go through passport control. The immigration officer who checked Francesco's identity card asked him all sorts of questions with the deepest professional indifference:

"Where have you come from?"

"Italy."

"Where are you going?"

"London."

"Do you have any criminal convictions?"

"No."

"Have you had any contagious diseases in the last three years?"

"No."

"Are you carrying any fresh meat, dairy or other animal products?"

Francesco looked around and patted his front and back pockets.

"Don't think so."

The man, who was used to that kind of humour, gave him back his ID.

In the end Francesco found himself on a train speeding from the coast to Victoria Station, with the flat English countryside opening up on either side of him.

On arriving in London, Francesco made his way to a bureau de change and exchanged the few remaining Dutch banknotes he had in his pockets. Coins could not be accepted, and the Indian behind the counter indulged in a little joke, telling him that there was a box in the tourist-information office where he could leave assorted foreign change for charity. All he got back was twelve pounds and thirty-five pence.

He tried to call Kyle from a phone box, but there was no answer. He ate a revolting tuna-and-cucumber sandwich, bought two postcards and sent one to her and one to his friend Leonardo, the aspiring writer, which just said, in Italian: "I made it to London – even on my own, you chicken!" For the reasonable sum of two pounds fifty he also got a copy of the Nicholson *Student's London Streetfinder*, to help him get around that vast metropolis stretching out for a hundred and sixty densely printed pages of roads and side streets.

When Francesco came out of Victoria Station, it was raining: not the summer downpours common in Italy, which get you drenched in an instant if you go out without an umbrella, but a patient, silent, sly, almost invisible drizzle that seeps into your bones. He set off all the same, heading straight for the hotel where he had agreed to meet up with Pierre the week before.

The hotel didn't look too far away on the *Streetfinder*, but – as he soon discovered – the scale was quite different from that of Italian city maps: he walked and walked and realized he had only gone a few hundred metres. After an hour's trek through the mizzle, however, he arrived in front of a four-star hotel on the Cromwell Road that seemed to promise rest for his aching feet and warmth for his numbed body. He looked at his watch, and although he was a bit early for his appointment with Pierre at three o'clock, he decided to go in.

The man at reception sized him up a couple of times when Francesco asked if there was any reservation in the name of Pierre Cordier. With a kind of nervous jerk, he turned his gaze from Francesco and started to scan a register, running down the page line by line with his finger.

"No, sir," he said with icy composure.

"No? But there must be a mistake. I have an appointment with him here today."

"Nothing in that name."

"Today is Tuesday – Tuesday the twenty-first, right?" Francesco asked, thinking for a moment that he may have got the dates mixed up.

"Yes, sir, today is the twenty-first, but I'm afraid we don't have any reservation for a Mr Cordier." He spelt out the last few words as if he were talking to someone hard of hearing.

Francesco tried to explain about the hotel vouchers – about Mansoor and the Munich hotel – but this seemed to make the situation even more confused. The man's expression of courteous displeasure gave way to mistrust, and mistrust to scepticism – but then one of his colleagues, presumably his boss, appeared at his side and said she remembered taking a booking under that name a few days earlier.

"There we go: Cordier," she said, flipping a page of the register. "You were right, sir. Mr Cordier had made a reservation for today, but he phoned on Saturday to change it to tomorrow."

"Tomorrow?"

"Yes, sir. The booking is for six days from tomorrow."

"So what shall I do?"

"Come back tomorrow, I suppose," the man said, with no trace of irony in his voice or in his expression.

"OK," Francesco said. "I'll come back tomorrow then."

"Very good, sir."

When Francesco came out of the hotel, it had stopped raining. He started to wander around at random, going from street to street, with no fixed destination in view. What could he do? The first thing that occurred to him was to go to the Italian embassy or consulate. He leafed through the *Streetfinder*, which on its final pages listed every kind of useful number, such as the British Pregnancy Advisory Centre, Alcoholics Anonymous and the British Acupuncture Association, but there was no ready-to-hand resource or facility for stray, penniless Italians in London.

He was walking past a modern-looking Catholic church. He climbed the steps and went inside. The nave was grey, dark, deserted, reminding him of an abandoned beehive. An old lady was arranging bouquets of flowers near the altar. Francesco went up to her and asked if she knew of any homeless shelters in the area.

"You should ask Father Jenkins," the old woman said. "He might know. He also has a few rooms at the back of the presbytery for seminary students. He's in the vestry now, if you want to talk to him."

Francesco went to see Father Jenkins, but his rooms turned out to be already occupied, and the nearest shelter was miles away. On the other hand, there was an old parishioner, Dr Marchetti, who had put up stranded Italian tourists several times, and might well be able to help on this occasion too. Francesco slouched to Marchetti's house, which was only a few streets away, but no one answered his insistent knocking. A woman from next door peered from her window and told him that she believed the old man was in hospital.

Francesco was in desperate need to rest his feet and take a shower, so he started looking for a youth hostel. The first place he came across was so filthy and squalid that the minute the Filipino at reception showed him the dormitory, he recoiled in horror. And for the privilege of sharing that cramped little room with five strangers he'd have had to pay eleven pounds.

"Des natting cheepa in London," the Filipino said, laughing. "You can check aynywhere, my friend."

So he'd have to resign himself to panhandling, or sleep under the bridges in the company of some old tramp. Another possibility was to take a train to Oxford and hope that Kyle would be around, or call his parents and ask them to find some way of sending him money. But Francesco could feel his brain turning to a mushy pulp. He just wanted to close his eyes, take off his shoes and forget about everything. Why couldn't God put out that dull, monotonous light up there? Why couldn't night fall right now and carry him away into some land of Cockaigne where rivers of camomile flowed and mountains of goose down stretched up to the sky?

For a brief instant his prayer was granted, and the light suddenly went out while he was lying on a park bench. But that refreshing sense of oblivion lasted only a moment: a shrill voice and a thin, sinewy hand shook him out of his torpor and forced him to reopen his eyes.

"What?" Francesco muttered, half asleep.

"What is the reason of this bivouac?" said a woman of around sixty, bending over him. Her face was plastered in make-up, and she was wearing a turban-style headscarf, like that of a Sikh.

"Huh?" he said, still dozy and bleary-eyed.

"What is the reason of this bivouac?" repeated the woman.

"Sorry, what do you mean?"

"Why are you sleeping on bench? This is where I sit to feed food to pigeons."

Francesco told her that he'd just arrived after a long journey and that he didn't have a place to sleep for the night.

"No place to sleep for night…" whispered the woman as if to herself, gazing up at the sky.

Francesco sat up and scrutinized her, starting with her head and moving down to her toes. To judge from the threadbare turban held together by a tuppenny-ha'penny brooch, the heavy make-up around her eyes and on her lips, the stained and ripped little jacket, the plastic bags that she was clutching, all bulging with scraps of paper and empty cans, and the down-at-heel shoes peeping out from under her thin cotton trousers, she might have just slipped away from a nearby lunatic asylum.

"No place for sleeping…" she repeated to herself, still gazing upwards. "If you like, you can stay for night… in daughter's flat…" she added with a crazed smile.

"Well, I am not sure I can—" Francesco began.

"I charge only five pounds per night," the woman interrupted him. "Daughter say I must not take strangers in house. She is lawyer. I tell her I only take good boys who don't smoke or play football. Pope disapprove of smoking and playing football. You don't smoke or play football?"

"Me? No."

"Then you are good boy. Please pay five pounds."

"Pay? Now?"

"Yes, before going to house. I must buy milk for breakfast and for cat."

Francesco gave her his last five-pound note and followed her. After ten minutes or so they arrived in front of one of the countless Victorian houses that stretched down the broad streets of that area. From the outside, there was nothing peculiar about it, apart from a sign that had been put up in the ground-floor window, saying: "NO POLL TAX".

The woman led Francesco down a steep flight of iron steps, and they came to a white door, bolted and padlocked, its paint all peeling.

"Key... key... Where did I put key? Ah yes, I go up and take it."

And the woman left him there waiting for another twenty minutes. When she was back, she explained that she had called her daughter and told her about him.

"I said you are good boy and don't smoke or play football, but she say she will call police if I don't answer phone tonight." She gave a mad laugh. "She worry about mother."

The woman had brought a glass of milk on a rusty tin tray and a bundle of old photos. She placed the tray on the rotting remains of a chair next to the door and gave the glass to Francesco, who thanked her and drank the milk in one long gulp.

"This is picture of me and husband on wedding day," the woman said, showing Francesco the photos. "Husband is dead for twenty years. This is premiere of *King Lear* at National Theatre. He played Fool. This is daughter Anja when she is seven, and this is son, Andrew. He work in New York now. He is famous doctor."

When she finally opened the door, Francesco's nose twitched at the musty stench that emerged. A pitch-black room yawned in front of them: the darkness seemed to soak up the faint light of dusk that came filtering in through the windows and the door. The woman moved ahead with assurance, escorting him through the various rooms and warning him that there was no electricity or running water, because they'd been cut off a few years before.

"Anja say: what is point of paying bills if flat is never used?"

Francesco followed her mechanically, bumping from time to time into a piece of furniture or some other dust-encrusted object lying on the floor or strewn around. In the end they reached the master bedroom, a kind of mausoleum lined with wooden panels and overflowing with heavy furniture.

"This is room where husband died," the woman announced.

"OK."

On the massive four-poster bed that reigned in the middle of the room, Francesco thought he could still make out the vague imprint of the dead man's body.

After giving him two old candle ends and a matchbox, the woman bade him goodnight and left. Once he was alone, Francesco took off his shoes, ran a hand over the bristly red blanket to see how dusty it was and gingerly climbed onto the creaky bed, laying his head on the pillow. He soon drifted off, and was fast asleep when the loud ring of a telephone made him jump. For over an hour he heard the muffled high notes of the woman's voice upstairs, and long silences punctuated by mad laughter. He fell asleep again, but at three o'clock in the morning he was woken up by the whooshing of a vacuum cleaner being dragged about on the wooden floor above him. This lasted for at least another hour, and when it stopped, Francesco could still hear for a long time the heavy thump of the woman's feet as she walked around restlessly in her flat.

Dawn finally broke, and he got up feeling more tired and sleepy than he had when he went to bed. It was a bright day outside, and a dim light trickled in through the grated windows of the basement. The bedroom's en-suite bathroom was "one of those sweet retreats which humane men erect for the accommodation of spiders". A large cockroach was squatting by the toilet bowl, and the washbasin was full almost to the brim with a brownish substance in which hairs, dead flies and mosquitoes floated. The living room was dominated by a leopard-skin sofa on which lay a jumble of old records, cushions, books, stools and other objects of uncertain use. On the walls were a few posters of British pop groups unknown to him – on the floor, little pots with dried-up plants in them. The kitchen was strewn with empty beer cans and broken bottles, and numerous unwashed plates and glasses were stacked in the sink.

Francesco went back into the living room, where from a rickety wooden bookcase he plucked mouldy copies of *Good Wives*, *Night of the Jaguar* and *The World Is Full of Divorced Women*, while from a built-in cupboard at the top slid a heap of risqué magazines from the Seventies, full of half-naked women, saucy stories and ridiculous Letters to the Editor – stuff that would now make his ten-year-old cousin smirk with derision, but that must have come with a whiff of forbidden fruit back then.

It was around eight when he tried to get out of the flat. The door, however, had been locked and bolted from the outside and, as the windows were protected by solid iron grates, there was no question of climbing out through them. Francesco thought this must be a precaution suggested by the woman's daughter and tried to fight down a rising sense of panic.

He waited for half an hour, then an hour, hoping the woman would come again with her rusty tin tray carrying a glass of milk, but time passed and she did not turn up. There was total silence upstairs. Perhaps she was asleep – perhaps she was wandering the streets of London collecting rubbish.

"Hello?..." Francesco called out, cautiously at first, then louder, but there was no response.

He picked up a broomstick from the kitchen and tapped on the ceiling.

"Hello?... Hello?..."

But nothing moved and not a sound came from upstairs. He looked around to see if there was another way out. Behind a double stack of boxes he noticed a white door, which he un-latched with some difficulty. He could not open it completely, but managed to squeeze through it and found himself at the bottom of a dark staircase. He went up, and reached another door. Luckily, it was not locked, so he opened it and stepped in.

"Is anybody there?" he shouted.

The flat was clean, uncluttered. There was a gentle smell of lavender in the air. The walls were hung with fine oil paintings and ornamental mirrors. Precious vases and a silver clock stood on the marble mantelpiece.

Francesco crossed the living room with circumspection and tried to open the front door, but it was locked. He walked over to the front bay window, and was unscrewing its lock when he felt something soft brush against his leg. His knees went slack and he almost toppled onto the floor. Looking down, he saw a black cat rubbing itself against his calf, purring away.

"Bad cat," Francesco hissed, reaching down to stroke its back. "You felines have such a great sense of timing…"

He finally managed to open the window and found his escape, sliding down the wall and landing in front of the door of the basement flat, careful not to be seen by anyone, but scratching his forearm and straining his ankle in the process. He limped up the iron staircase and, after casting a guarded look around, stepped onto the street. Half an hour later, as a weightless rain began to fall again, he was outside the hotel on the Cromwell Road.

At around three, after a nerve-racking wait, Francesco saw a red Maserati pull up outside the entrance to the hotel. A familiar figure of piratical appearance slithered out of the car and headed for the main door.

"Pierre!" Francesco called out.

Pierre turned round and, lifting his sunglasses, darted a sidelong glance at him, before saying:

"You're here? Do me a favour: take my luggage in while I check in." And he threw the car keys to him in a perfect arc. Francesco managed to catch them just before they hit him in the face. In the meantime Pierre had slipped inside.

When Francesco dragged the cases in, Pierre came up to him and said, "Good to see you, pal. Do me another favour – take them up to the room. Here's the key. Did you have a good journey?"

Francesco turned a frowning gaze on him.

"Man, you look like a murder scene. Go on, take a shower. We're going out tonight… you don't wanna stink… I'll go and park the car in the meantime... See you in a few minutes..."

And he was off. A porter asked Francesco if he needed any help with the cases, but Francesco shook his head and called the lift.

The room was splendid, draped with soft furnishings. Francesco went to the bathroom and took a hot shower. He then drew the curtains, stretched out on one of the beds and tried to relax, closing his eyes and surrendering to the vague drift of his thoughts.

He woke up hugging his pillow and with the acrid smell of smoke in his nostrils. He jerked his head up: Pierre was sitting at a tea table in front of him, enjoying a cigarette as he scribbled something on a piece of paper.

"What are you writing?" Francesco asked.

Pierre turned to look at him. "'The Sleep of the Just: An Ode'. Had a nice little nap, have we?" He glanced at his watch: "You clocked up just under two hours."

Francesco sat up. "Really?" he said, then yawned.

The curtains were opened, and he was obliged to shield his eyes with his arm. "Why did you change the hotel booking?" he asked, getting up from bed.

"Oh, sorry pal, I had to. My life's a bit complicated at the moment. Hope I didn't cause you any inconvenience?"

"Well, apart from having to spend the night locked up in the basement of a Polish psycho, with no light or running water, everything else was fine."

"You could have checked in here."

Francesco explained that he had no money on him, having lost his bag before reaching England.

"Money, money," scoffed Pierre. "Why do you still worry about money? If you don't pay, someone will always pick up the tab for you. You haven't learnt my lesson, then?"

Francesco shrugged.

"So what was Amsterdam like?" Pierre asked, stubbing his cigarette in the ashtray.

"Not very memorable."

"No? What did you get up to there?"

"Nothing."

"Nothing?"

"Why, what do you know?"

"About what?"

"About what I did there, what happened."

"I don't know anything about anything."

"You sure you don't know anything?"

"What's wrong with you? Did you get a blow on your head?" Pierre gave a nervous laugh.

"I did, actually. I did."

Francesco walked back to the bathroom and got dressed. When he came out, Pierre was waiting for him by the door.

"You peckish?"

"Well, I've been on hunger strike since yesterday, so I wouldn't mind a bite."

"Let's go to Trulli, then. You won't get a better plate of *spaghetti alla carbonara* this side of the English Channel. And the manager, Peppe, is an old pal of mine – we won't have to pay."

Around twenty minutes later, having parked the Maserati in a "Residents Only" car park with menacing wheel-clamping signs, they arrived at a small restaurant off the Fulham Road. As soon as they went in, a couple of waiters rushed up to them.

"Howyadoing, Pierre?"

"How's tricks? Long time no see."

The restaurant was full, but soon they were sitting at a table with the menu in their hands. As they examined the culinary specialities on offer, out jumped a kind of satyr, a Toby jug of a man with a round bald head, glasses perched on the tip of his nose, long limbs that were out of proportion with the thickset body from which they dangled, and a set of nervous twitches that made him jerk his neck every other second.

"And 'ow are w-w-w-we a-keepin', gentlemen?" Peppe Maria Trulli said in a reedy little voice. "You've become a f-f-foreigner, *che cazz'*."

Every word, every gesture shot from his person like a bullet from a well-oiled machine gun, except when the tics gained the upper hand and his neck gave an unexpectedly powerful jerk, forcing his rapid rattle to fizzle out.

Peppe gave Pierre a long and affectionate hug, then sat next to him and started to shower him with questions, nudges, nods and winks, jokes, sudden shrieks, bursts of laughter and nervous twitches. Even before the antipasti arrived, one of the waiters brought a bottle of Grifo and one of Tocai that "would set the angels singing and dancing in Paradise". After ten minutes, what with the wine and Peppe's chatter, Francesco's head was already spinning.

Then dinner began. For starters they served a dish of broccoli and potatoes fresh from the oven, accompanied by broiled vegetables, *favetta pugliese* and pan-fried porcini mushrooms with garlic and parsley, followed by grilled Normandy artichokes and veal carpaccio with balsamic vinegar. To prevent the occurrence of hiccups, there soon arrived a bottle of Verdicchio dei Castelli di Jesi, which one of Peppe's distant relatives – a certain Arcangelo, from the Marche region – brought him every year in person, in five-litre jerrycans.

The *primo* was made up of three generous *assaggini*: *pappardelle al sugo di lepre*, *risotto ai funghi di bosco* and *cavatelli alla rucola con ricotta affumicata*. By now Francesco was pretty stuffed, but this was only the start of the proceedings: Peppe drew on the resources of his kitchen to surprise them with more and more delicacies. Francesco let out a sigh and slumped back in his chair when he saw the waiters advance with three huge trays bearing the main course, which consisted of *agnello alla scottadito*, paired with wild-boar sausages in a spicy sauce and oxtail, together with their relevant side dishes.

Pierre ate with beastly appetite. He knocked back glass after glass of wine and smoked between each course, chatting away and roaring with laughter as he and Peppe reminisced about the good old times.

"Remember the trick you played on that old Kraut?" said Pierre, puffing out and narrowing his Levantine eyes. "The face he made when he found your little 'present' in his dish?"

And Peppe doubled up with laughter, with a spasmodic jerk of his neck.

For dessert they brought tiramisù and profiteroles, then came the espresso and an indeterminate number of bottles of liqueur on a trolley. The rest of the evening was shrouded in the dense smoke of Pierre's cigarettes. Peppe led the way to a private room for a quick game of poker with his friend, ten pounds a chip, free raise. Every so often the waiters would come to watch a hand, leaving table number six's *parmigiana*

to get cold, or ignoring the lady who had asked for another
bottle of "spark-a-lìnne" mineral water. Francesco sank ever
deeper into his quilted seat, coming to with a start every now
and again when he heard the sputtering of the machine gun
or Pierre's dry bark:

"Lucky bastard."

"Check."

"Three bitches."

"Main street."

"T-ta-ten graands!"

They reeled out at about midnight. They made a move in the
direction of the car, but Pierre had drunk so much that they
decided to jump in a cab. Half an hour later they climbed out
at the entrance to a club in the heart of the West End, which
at this time of night was swarming with people. The bouncer
at the door touched fists with Pierre, whispered something in
his ear, flashed a white smile and let them in.

Inside, the bluish light revealed high stools and low couches
on which hazy, sinuous, glittering shapes were murmuring
and drinking. Pierre and Francesco came to a room lit up by
projecting lamps in the corners.

"That's Jerry Byngo over there," said Pierre, with a vague
pointing gesture, "the lead singer of Kiss My R's. You see the
guy he's talking to? He's the guitarist from Nick & the Antipope.
Used to be with the Kinky Monkeys before that."

Francesco nodded.

Pierre seemed to be a well-known figure in the establishment.
People waved at him, came up to pay their respects, and at one
point an anorexic young girl in a miniskirt, braying drunk,
threw herself on him and kissed him on the lips.

"Hey, man!" shouted a voice from one of the couches. "I didn't know you were around."

The voice belonged to a moon-faced, white-haired, goateed man of about forty, dressed entirely in black except for a pink tie, and wearing a white fedora and two earrings in each ear. It transpired he was the director of a major art gallery in Bond Street. He was there with his staff and a group of young artists as a coda to the celebrations of the opening of a new photography exhibition.

Pierre bantered with him and told him he would go and see him at his gallery the following day, without fail, then moved on to join another bunch of people nearby and disappeared. Francesco was offered a chair, and a few moments later he discovered he was holding a very exotic and very alcoholic cocktail in his hand.

"So where are you from?" the director of the art gallery, Dave, asked him, after a round of introductions. "And how do you know Pierre?"

Francesco felt his tongue wag and chatter away as it related a few things about himself, his travels and how he had bumped into Pierre. Then, as more drinks were conjured up on the table and Dave and the others continued to talk, Francesco listened on with a vacant expression, smiling and nodding.

"What is he? An art dealer, a collector?" one of the artists asked Dave.

"Bit of both." Then Dave whispered: "Someone told me he's worth a few hundred mill. He owns one per cent of London."

"How did he make his money?"

"Steel. His father was a foundry owner. He's related to the Rockefellers or the Rothschilds, apparently, by way of an aunt.

He's got properties all over Europe and America. And I have heard that he's gay."

One by one, Dave and the others left, and Francesco remained alone on the couch with one of the gallery assistants, a fair-headed girl called Chloe, talking about art, literature and life in that abstract and idealistic way that only intoxicated young creatures are ever able to capture. Chloe was one of those rare people who can wear their beauty, intelligence and joie de vivre lightly, without making you feel bad for trying to soak it up, and Francesco felt a natural affinity for her. As closing time beckoned, they exchanged their contact details and she left.

After that, Francesco's memories became blurred. He remembered his limp body being dragged out onto the street; then, after the noise and scattered blaze of Trafalgar Square, he felt two fingers worming their way down his throat as he stuck his head over the parapet of a bridge on the Thames, his soul slipping out to sea, Big Ben and the Houses of Parliament lit up on the horizon, the leathery aroma of a car seat, his head under the shower, an awkward fall, a bleeding gum, the warmth of the bed, lights out, fireflies flickering through the room, darkness.

The following morning he woke up flat on his belly at the far end of the bed, with the pillow over his head and his arms spread out in a cross, as if someone had stabbed him in the back and left him there inert. He hauled himself up and looked around. A humming sound could be heard from the bathroom. After probing the aching gum with his tongue, he called out, "Pierre!"

A foam-covered face popped out of the bathroom.

"Hello Lazarus!"

"Good morning."

"Good afternoon, you mean. You hungover? Drink some orange juice: it'll kill your headache."

Francesco followed his advice.

When he reappeared, Pierre was already fully dressed.

"Any plans for today?" he asked, adjusting his tie in front of the mirror.

"I want to go to Oxford to see a friend."

"Good. I'm tied up with a few meetings here, so I guess I'll see you later tonight. Do you need any money?"

"Well, if I could borrow ten or fifteen quid…"

"No worries," Pierre said, reaching into his pocket and producing a fat wad of notes. "Take fifty… take a hundred."

"It's too much."

"Never say no when someone's offering you money."

"OK. Thanks."

"If you come with me to pick up the car, I can give you a lift to the coach station."

"Sure."

Soon they were in a black cab speeding towards the Fulham Road. Pierre said that he was fed up of having to travel so much for work, and that he missed the freedom of his younger years. Then he launched into one of his rants against the rules, constraints and fetters of modern civilization.

"Like the poet wrote," Pierre said, as he paid the cab driver and brought his invective to a climax, "a body's been slipped over the heart, and over the body a shirt – and some idiot has created cuffs and collars and starched them stiff and started ironing them…" He scoffed. "You see, property, law and religion are just a scarecrow erected by the rich and powerful.

You just try to do something you're not supposed to do and out pops a copper, a priest or a pettifogger."

"Or a clamper," Francesco said, pointing at the front wheel of his friend's Maserati.

Pierre's face blanched. He blinked, nodded and, swearing to himself, walked over to his car. In the meantime, sitting on the low wall of an adjacent construction site, three builders were sniggering as they looked on and drank their coffees. One of them, seeing Pierre's dumbfounded expression, shouted, "Have you been clamped, mate?"

"What?"

"You been clamped?"

"Looks like it," said Pierre. He walked round the car three or four times, then shouted: "You don't have an angle-grinder on you, do you?"

"Nah, we don't do angle-grinders," said the oldest of the three.

"You wanna use hammer, chisel and crowbar," said the one in the middle, a kind of living tattoo. "It's a pain in the arse, but it works."

"The best way," said the third one, the youngest, "is to hack-saw one of the joints in the chains and then jemmy apart."

"I'd let air from the tyre and pull the top bar away from the wheel."

"Nah. Won't work with this one: the wheel's too big."

And so it went on for a few more minutes. Eventually, the labourers came over and inspected the wheel clamp with pro-fessional care.

"What you want is a drill with a titanium or a cobalt bit," the man with tattoos explained. "You just drill the lock mechanism here – pop."

"A seven- or eight-mil bit should do, Jim."

The youngest builder went over to their van and came back with a cordless drill and some bits. Pierre didn't hang around, and started to drill through the lock – and soon the clamp fell down, like the head of a vanquished beast, under the approving looks of the three builders.

Scudding along at sixty miles per hour across the crowded streets of Fulham and Chelsea, Pierre seemed to have regained his chutzpah. As he overtook a car on the left and sped through a red light, he said with gleaming, mischievous eyes: "Nobody – *nobody* puts a clamp on me!"

7

Oxford

ONCE HE ARRIVED in Oxford, Francesco bought new under-wear, a T-shirt and jeans, a shoulder bag and a pair of shoes from M&S, then he got changed and tried to call Kyle from a phone box.

"She's not in," the person who answered the phone said. "She'll be back later."

"What time?"

"Dunno. Six? Seven?"

"Can you tell her that Francesco called?"

"No sweat."

The line went dead.

Francesco whiled away a couple of hours admiring the soft colours, elegant shapes and towering spires of the old town's buildings. Then, after eating a sandwich in the quadrangle of the Bodleian Library, he got a map from a tourist office and made his way to Kyle's address, situated in a cul-de-sac off the Banbury Road in Summertown, around twenty minutes' walk from the city centre.

When he arrived there, he was surprised to find that she was living in a large Edwardian house, not in some cheap student flat. He rang the bell, and as the door opened he realized, from the noise inside, that there was some sort of party or dinner going on.

"I'm a friend of Kyle's," Francesco said. "Is she in?"

"Hang on a sec." The boy at the door turned and shouted: "Kyle! Kyle!"

Then he went in again, leaving Francesco there.

A few minutes passed before Kyle came to the door. Her eyes were red, and her mascara was smudged with tears.

"Hiya," she said, with an uncomfortable smile.

"Kyle, what's going on?"

"Nothing," she said, and wiped a tear that was about to roll down her face. "Nothing. It's just that… it's just that this is not a very good time. I'm sorry."

"Did you receive my card?"

"Yes, thank you."

"Is there anything—"

"No, thanks. I'll explain to you some other time. Now it's not—"

The door was pried open from behind her, and a spindly young man with a sparse reddish beard and frizzy red hair appeared.

"So you're Kyle's famous Italian friend?" he said, with a grin on his face and a strong Irish accent. "Come on in, we were all dying to meet you."

"Oh, Dan!" Kyle gave the boy a shove and walked back inside.

Dan tilted his head and made an inviting gesture to go in with the palms of his hands. Francesco stepped inside and followed him, closing the door. Half a dozen people were sitting around the living-room table, which was cluttered with beer cans, half-empty bottles of wine, dirty plates and plastic boxes with the remains of a takeaway dinner. When Francesco entered the room, they stopped their drinking and chatting.

"Hiya."

As he took his place between a blonde girl and the boy who had opened the door, Francesco noticed that Kyle, still sobbing, had taken refuge in the kitchen, where the radio was playing 'Losing My Religion' by R.E.M.

"Guys, this is Francesco," said Dan, who was sitting across from him. Then, moving his arm clockwise and pointing round the table, he added: "Francesco, this is Steve, Deb, Sarah, John, Pete, Sam – and I'm Dan. Help yourself with the food if you're hungry: I think they're finished with it. Can I get you a drink?"

"I'm all right, thanks. Just a glass of water."

"Oooh, save water – drink wine."

"All right, I'll have a drop of wine. What's happened to Kyle?"

"Oh, don't worry." Dan made a dismissive gesture. "She's just having a bad day."

"A bad day?"

"Yeah, she got up on the wrong side of life this morning, you know what I mean? It could be physiological. Might have something to do with the moon, too."

Sarah, the girl sitting next to Francesco, giggled.

"So you met Kyle in Lund, she told me," Dan continued, pouring himself a large glass of red wine.

"I was passing by on my InterRail trip."

"I see. And how did you meet her?"

"We were just hanging out with some friends."

"You were just *hanging out* with some friends," Dan repeated, then had a long sip from his glass. "Your English is pretty good. You don't seem to have a strong Italian accent."

"I study English at university," Francesco said with an embarrassed smile.

"Oh, you do? And what is your area of study?"

"English literature and linguistics."

"Just like myself. So, what are your favourite English authors?"

"Well, it's difficult to say." He looked around and felt observed. "I suppose... Chaucer, Spenser, the Romantics..."

"Bah. No one reads that stuff any more in this country. Do you like Joyce?"

"I'm not too keen on Joyce."

"You're not?"

"Dan can recite the whole of *Finnegans Wake* backwards by heart," Steve said. Steve had a big nose and the smallest ears Francesco had ever seen on a human head.

"I can see some merit in that," said Francesco, nodding.

Dan stroked his beard and stared at Francesco for some time.

"You don't like *Ulysses*?" Dan asked. "Seriously? You don't think it's a masterpiece?"

"Certainly a *mastur*-piece."

Dan grinned and nodded. "What about living authors?"

"I don't read much contemporary fiction."

"You don't? Why?"

"Because, frankly, most of it is hardly worth the bother. It's all about *me*, *me*, *me*. The underlying message seems to be: 'I don't care about the past, I can see no point in the future, but fortunately for you, dear Reader, there is me here now, preening in a timeless mirror.'"

Dan drank off his wine and put the empty glass on the table.

"That's bullshit," he said, looking at the others, who seemed captivated by the debate, or perhaps just clouded with too much drink.

"Bullshit?" said Francesco.

"Yes, *mierda de toro*. And I can tell you that anything pre-twentieth century is a waste of time."

"Including Dante?"

"Dante's all right. I think he influenced Joyce and Beckett, didn't he?"

"That's just the point I was trying to make. Without the literature of the past the modernists are nothing. What do you think of Shakespeare?"

"Shakespeare's all right too, except he didn't write any of his works."

"No? Who did then?"

"Marlowe, or some Jewish woman. The real Shakespeare was a Sicilian Jew."

"I didn't know that."

"Well, you learn new things every day. What about literary criticism?"

"What about it?"

"Aren't you interested in literary theory?"

Francesco laughed. "The critics and I are, luckily, no friends."

"So you haven't read anything by Lacan or Derrida?"

"I'm afraid not. But I think I've read somewhere that Chomsky called Lacan 'an amusing and perfectly self-conscious charlatan'."

"Chomsky's an arsehole," Dan said. He then stood up and with slow movements disengaged himself from under the table and walked towards the kitchen.

"Dan's a Derrida scholar," whispered Sarah. "He's writing a deconstructive critique of twentieth-century comics."

"It's called *Structure, Sign and Ludus from Mickey Mouse to Asterix*," said Pete, hastening to hide his nose in his wineglass.

"Soon he'll be offered the Chair of Meta-drivel at the University of Barking," John chipped in.

Francesco gave a cautious smile. A heated exchange was heard in the kitchen, followed by the noise of drawers being opened and closed and the clunk of crockery and cutlery.

"Have you been to Oxford before?" asked Deb.

"No, this is my first time," said Francesco. "I'd only seen it through the eyes of Giordano Bruno."

"What do you make of it?"

"Well, I suppose it's changed quite a bit since then."

"Nah," John intervened. "It's not changed much. From the outside, maybe. But inside it's always the same old story: people bullshitting each other over a glass of beer."

Dan reappeared in the living room with a small plate, a fork and an opened can of peeled tomatoes. He sat down between Sam and Steve, placed the plate on the table and put the can on it, then lifted open the lid with the point of his fork and fished a whole tomato out of the tin.

"Sorry, disquisitions make me hungry," Dan said with a half-smile. He was about to take the first bite when Francesco said:

"Hey, hey, hey!"

Dan's fork stopped in mid-air.

"What?"

"You're not really eating it like that?"

"What do you mean?"

"That's only used in sauces: it can't be eaten uncooked."

"What are you talking about? I've had it many times. It's good for your health, for your gastrointestinal tract. You should try it."

"Dan only eats raw, unprocessed foods," Steve explained.

"Fruit and vegetables," Dan pointed out, taking the first bite of the tomato. "Meat is murder."

"Have you ever heard about botulism?" Francesco said.

"Who, the Dutch author?"

Everyone laughed.

"I am sure the cans are sterilized and pasteurized," Francesco added. "You can't call this food 'unprocessed'."

"It doesn't matter, Mr Mozzarella, so long as it's not cooked."

Francesco shook his head as Dan poured himself another glass of red wine and continued to eat.

At that point Kyle came into the room with a black bin liner and began to pick up the litter from the table.

"Don't worry, sweetheart," Dan said after she had cleared half the table, "I'll clean up later and take the bags to the recycling centre."

"I'm not your sweetheart," Kyle said with a cutting tone, thrusting two more empty cans in the refuse sack.

"All right." Pete placed his glass on the table and stood up, encouraging Sam to do the same. "I think we'd better be going. We've got stuff to sort out upstairs."

"Yeah, I'm going too," said Deb. "I'm supposed to be writing an essay."

After exchanging goodnight kisses and goodbyes, everyone retreated, leaving Dan, Kyle and Francesco alone in the living room.

"Well, I must be on my way too," Francesco said, trying to break the awkwardness of the situation. "It's getting late, and I've got to go back to London."

"You don't have to go back," Dan said with his acid grin, then took a long sip from his glass. "You can sleep in Kyle's room: I've just moved out, you know?"

"Dan and I are splitting up," Kyle said after a pause, flashing an icy stare at Dan.

"You are… splitting up? You were engaged?"

Kyle turned a frowning look on Francesco. "Naw. Course not. He was just my boyfriend."

Francesco could not see the difference, but nodded.

"So the coast is clear now," Dan said. "Best of luck, Mr Macaroni."

"No need to be nasty or sour, Dan," Kyle said.

"Sour? Why should I be sour? We've been together three years, we had a good time, we had great sex. I don't see any problem with getting up one morning and being told that I'm not loved any more and that there's some new Katzelmacher ready to slip into my shoes. I am a liberal, tolerant thinker – I believe in free trade and natural succession, you see? The King's dead – long live the King! Marriage and love are so nineteenth century. I don't give a damn who you've been screwing around with, and—"

Kyle reached across the table and slapped him in the face.

"Now, I knew you were a slapper, but *that* you should not have done," Dan cried out, massaging his cheek. "I can't stand physical violence." He raised his bulk from under the table and made a threatening move towards Kyle. Francesco stretched out his arm and intervened between them.

"Come on now, calm down," he said. "Calm down."

"You stay out of this," Dan said.

"Look, I'm sorry I came here today. I didn't mean to—"

"I said stay out of this."

"There's no need to get agitated. I'll be gone in a moment."

"Don't provoke me."

"I'm not provoking you, I'm just trying—"

But Francesco could not finish his words: Dan had reached for the tomato can and poured its contents onto his head.

"Why did you do that?" shrieked Kyle, then pushed Dan off-balance so that he stumbled back against the wall.

Pete was the first to rush from upstairs, followed by the others.

"Whoa, whoa!" he shouted, entering the living room.

"It's OK, it's only tomato juice," Francesco said.

"What a mess," Steve said from behind the door, looking at Francesco's clothes and the floor around him. "Man, you've drunk too much plonk."

"Sorry," stammered Dan, before slumping onto a chair.

A few minutes later, after getting changed, Francesco was on his way back to the city centre to catch the London coach, with Kyle walking by his side. She was still shaken and untalkative, and often ran a nervous hand through her hair to brush the fringe off her brow.

"I'm sorry for having caused trouble," Francesco said.

"Don't say that: it's not your fault. He saw your postcard this morning and we had a big row. I couldn't lie to him any more. I just don't feel the same way about him as I did before leaving for Sweden. I've lost interest in him and his balls-to-the-wall ideas. I've lost faith."

They continued to walk in silence until they reached the main bus station. When the coach for London arrived and opened its doors, they hugged each other for a brief moment and kissed on the cheek.

"Will you be all right going back alone at this time of night?" Francesco said.

"Don't worry, I'll get a cab."

"Dan's not going to bother you, is he?"

"He's harmless. He's just a big child."

"Will you ask one of the girls to sleep in your room tonight?"

"I know how to take care of myself."

"OK."

The other passengers had boarded, and the coach was ready to leave.

"Tomorrow I'm busy," Kyle said, "but I'll try to come to London on Saturday."

"That would be great. Just give me a ring at the hotel."

"And I'll bring you your clothes. Hopefully the stains will come out."

"Don't worry. You can throw them away."

"Next time lucky?"

"Next time lucky. Definitely."

"Promise?"

"Promise."

As the coach drove away into the darkness of the Oxford countryside and careered towards London, Francesco thought again of Kyle's auburn hair – her tearful blue eyes, her beautiful smile, the slight Irish lilt in her voice – and felt, perhaps for the first time in his life, that he was leaving a part of himself behind.

8

London

THE NEXT DAY, Pierre and Francesco drove around crowded streets clogged with traffic, visiting antique shops and galleries in Bond Street and Cork Street, meeting wealthy individuals with names like Stematsky, Al Baktoum, Itoyama, shady businessmen with golden rings and orange comb-overs, rich widows with strange plumed hats.

In the afternoon, after a lavish lunch at Scalini's, they followed a keen estate agent – one of those "things that ceaselessly speak" – from a Knightsbridge property to another one in Chelsea or Kensington as Pierre was shown some of the most expensive flats and houses on the market.

"This one's a real bargain, just over a mill," the woman was saying. "It's got four bedrooms, two bathrooms, Jacuzzi, designer kitchen, double glazing, communal garden, resident day porterage and private parking. If you're thinking of doing a quick flip, you can't get anything better than this." She lowered the voice to a whisper: "The owner is relocating abroad. He's desperate to move out."

"A distressed seller?"

"Suicidal."

"Mmm. It's a bit too small for what I had in mind," was Pierre's final comment. "I think we'll have to go up a notch or two."

"No problem at all," said the agent, brightening up and getting even more excited. "How are you set up for tomorrow?"

They dined at Cecconi's, in Mayfair, had drinks at the Groucho, then went from one party to another and returned to the hotel in the early hours.

When Francesco woke up on the Saturday morning, Pierre was again sitting at the small table near the window with a pen in one hand and a cigarette in the other.

"Haven't you finished your ode?" Francesco asked.

"That'll be a work in progress for as long as you're around."

"What are you writing?"

Pierre lit up his cigarette and took a long drag.

"A novel."

"I didn't know you were a novelist."

"That's just one of my hats."

"Are you a published author?"

"Oh yeah."

"How can you find time to write a novel?"

"How? You just have to make time. 'No one gets fame or wealth, my master said, taking it easy in a feather bed.'"

"You're good at cribbing poetry too."

The phone rang, and Pierre went over to answer it.

"Sounds like you have a female visitor waiting for you in reception," he announced.

"My friend from Oxford," said Francesco, jumping off the bed. "She's already here? What time is it?"

"It's just gone eleven. Do you need the room for a bit of lo-comotion? I'll be off in ten minutes."

"Thanks for the thought, but I think we'll just start the day with a walk."

"Just trying to be helpful."

Francesco took a shower, got dressed, said bye to Pierre and rushed downstairs. But he was surprised to see that the person waiting for him in reception wasn't Kyle. It took him a moment to realize that the beautiful girl with tied-back blond hair and a golden wisp dangling over her eyes was the one he had met the other day at the nightclub.

"Hi Francesco."

"Chloe?"

The girl smiled. "You seem surprised. We said we'd go to the National Gallery together, remember?"

He didn't. "Of course, of course. Sorry, I'm still a bit groggy. I had another late night with Pierre yesterday."

They stepped out into the sunshine and made their way to the Underground station. Getting off at Leicester Square, they walked down Charing Cross Road towards Trafalgar Square. They spent over two hours in the National Gallery, gawping at the masterpieces of the Italian Renaissance. Then, after a quick browse in the gallery bookshop, they headed to Covent Garden, pausing for a while to gaze in curiosity at the assorted mime artists, acrobats and comedians who were showing off their skills around the square.

They spotted a free table outside a brasserie nearby, and or-dered first a glass of wine and then some food. The sunshine was beating down on them, and Francesco sat back on his chair and listened to Chloe as she talked, observing all her small expressions and gestures: if Kyle was a flickering fire, Chloe was the wind humming among the treetops; if Kyle was a wild cat that could scratch you at times, even when you tried to stroke her, Chloe was a gazelle leaping with grace among meadows and grassland.

"My head's still spinning with all those Raphaels and Titians," Chloe was saying. "What would the world be like without you Italians?"

"A better place, probably."

"Why do you say that?"

"Because the descendants of Raphael and Titian think that it's more useful and honourable to clean out cesspools than create works of art."

"You're being harsh to your country."

"You think so? You should try and live there. Perhaps if you knew of Tangentopoli, the mafia killings and Berlusconi you'd think otherwise. Today's Italians are farther removed from their past glories—"

"Than the modern Greeks from the ancient Greeks."

"No: a more accurate comparison would be present-day England from Stonehenge, or modern France from Lascaux. Italy is regressing: we're just at the start of our new Middle Ages now."

"At least you have a democracy."

"Well, I'm not sure about that. Most of the people I know are still praying for another 'Man of Destiny'. And we'll probably get one before long."

"What do you make of England and our royal family?"

"Oh, I wouldn't dare to say a word."

"Why?"

"You know what Leonardo da Vinci once said? 'I do not meddle with anything to do with the royals, because they are the perfection of truth.'"

"Come on, don't be cagey. I promise you won't end up in the Tower of London."

"Honestly, I don't know. I haven't formed an idea. Perhaps I wouldn't be able to form one even if I lived here for twenty or thirty years. I guess it would all still remain impenetrable to me."

After their meal, they strolled around and continued to talk for another hour or so. Francesco described some of the places he had visited over the past two weeks, making sure to avoid any mention of Kyle and his trip to Oxford, while Chloe revealed that she wanted to leave her job at the art gallery and take a year off to travel around Europe or Australia with a friend.

By now they had reached one of the entrances to Tottenham Court Road Tube station, and amid the bustle and noise of people streaming past in both directions, the moment to separate had come.

"It's been a lovely day," said Chloe.

"Really lovely. Maybe we could go out again tomorrow…"

"Tomorrow I'll be working at the gallery. Perhaps next week?"

"I'm not sure how long I'm going to stay in London. Let's swap addresses, you never know."

And they scrawled their details on a piece of paper.

"Ah well," said Chloe, "must be off now. It was good to see you."

"Chloe…"

"Yes?"

"Nothing… it was a lovely day."

"Yes, it was really lovely."

And at that moment, Francesco felt that unless he made a move he would never see her again. So he closed his eyes and brushed a kiss not on her cheeks, but on that area so little explored by the poets of love, extending from the upper lip to the root of the nose, that area covered by an invisible down and furrowed by a small groove, where a hundred contrasting emotions do battle with one another, making the mouth curl into a smile or a grimace.

Chloe was taken aback by the eloquence of that simple gesture. She started and backed away, as if scared, but then she smiled and stepped out towards the entrance to the Underground. Once inside, she turned and smiled at him again, then waved and disappeared down the stairs into the crowd.

Francesco skipped along to Leicester Square and got onto a westbound Piccadilly Line train. When he arrived back at the hotel, he saw, behind the reception desk, the imperturbable man who had welcomed him the first time.

"Has anyone left any messages for me?" said Francesco.

The man looked at him as if he had just been asked what colour moon flies are.

"Room number?"

"512."

"No messages," the man said after a short pause.

"No messages?"

"No."

"Weird."

He went up to his room, and when he opened the door he had the impression that a burglar was at work. In fact, it was Pierre who was scrambling all his clothes into his suitcases.

"What's happening?" Francesco asked. "You're leaving?"

Pierre stopped for a moment and turned to look at him.

"Oh, you're back? Good. Look, I'm sorry, I've gotta go. I have some problems. Cash-flow problems.

"Cash-flow problems?"

"Well, I was eating again at Trulli's today, and that devil, Peppe, comes to me and goes: 'You c-c-c-can't go away likke dis, eh?'" – he imitated Peppe's neck jerks – "'Just a quick leetle game of a-poker...' So he takes me into the back room and makes me try a few bottles of liqueur his cousin has smuggled in from Romania. So it was just a little drop here and just another little drop there and I found myself with a hand of cards and a pile of poker chips in front of me. He wiped me out."

"He wiped you out?"

"Totally."

"Can't you take some cash out of a bank, or an ATM?"

Pierre stopped again.

"You're a genius. I didn't think about that." He shook his head and closed the suitcases. "My credit cards have stopped working for good."

"Why?"

There was another pause.

"It's complicated. Very complicated."

"What is?"

"My cash situation. My monetary arrangements. My budgetary infrastructures. Don't worry, it'll be all right. But I have to go now."

Francesco sat on the edge of the bed.

"So what are you going to do about the hotel bill?"

"Me? I'm not going to do anything. Not my problem."

"Who's gonna pay, then?"

"Can't pay, won't pay."

"Very funny. Come on, seriously: this would be a runner too many."

"Look, I told you already that you should stop worrying about money. If you don't pay—"

"Someone else is gonna pick up the tab. So who's gonna pay this time?"

Pierre thought for a moment, then said, with a piratical smile:

"Vanessa."

"Vanessa?"

"Yeah, Vanessa, my lovely wife."

"She won't mind?"

"No, she won't. She'll pay up, believe me." He winked. "She'll be only too happy. Give her a call, here's the number." He scribbled something on the hotel paper.

"Why don't you call her?"

"Oh I'll give her a call later – in fact, I need to talk to her. But I'm in a bit of a rush now – they're bringing my car round. Sort this out for me, will you?" Pierre gave him a double pat on his arm. "Are you stopping off in Paris?"

"Well, I was planning to, on the way back, yeah."

"I tell you what, then. Clean up this little mess here and jump on the first train to Paris. We'll meet there tomorrow afternoon, OK?"

"Where?"

"Let's meet at" – Pierre gave this some thought – "let's meet at Père Lachaise, at 3 p.m. By Chopin's grave."

"Chopin's grave?"

"Yeah, what's wrong with that?"

"Well, I don't usually meet people at tombs."

Pierre grinned. He took his suitcases and made towards the door, then turned.

"Much appreciated, pal," he said. "I'll make it up to you. *Hasta la vista!*"

And he was gone. Francesco jumped to his feet and peered out of the room, calling out after him: "Pierre! Hey, Pierre!"

But the only sound that came back was the clang of the lift's doors, followed by a metallic purr.

"This must be a joke," he whispered to himself, shaking his head, "some sort of stupid, elaborate joke."

He sat down again on the edge of the bed, and the room felt like it was rocking. People's faces, images, thoughts, questions, scenarios floated and burst around him. Should he get in touch with Vanessa? He was supposed to tell her about the stolen package too. Should he call Kyle or Chloe? Or his parents? Should he meet with Pierre in Paris the following day? He could try to sneak away without paying. After all, the hotel didn't have his passport or credit-card details, and the booking had been made in Pierre's name. But that, for some reason, didn't seem right.

He went over to the phone and dialled Vanessa's number. She picked up the receiver on the second ring.

"Vanessa? It's Francesco here."

She didn't seem surprised to hear him, and asked in a level voice: "How are you?"

Francesco told her in short, syncopated sentences, that he was more or less all right, except that – well – he had lost her package in Amsterdam and needed her help to get out of the new predicament Pierre had placed him in.

"I know."

"You know?"

"I know about Amsterdam. I'm sorry," she said. "I didn't mean to get you into trouble. I'll explain everything later. And I'll take care of the hotel bill, don't worry." Her tone was sad, weary, almost dejected. "Where is he now?"

"He's left."

"Where did he go?"

"I'm not sure. But we are supposed to meet in Paris tomorrow."

He told her about their afternoon appointment at Père Lachaise cemetery.

"I'll try to be there. I must talk to him before…" She trailed off.

"He said he'd call you," murmured Francesco, filling the pause.

"He won't call me," was Vanessa's response. "He's… he'll…"

"Look," Francesco said. "I don't think it's a good idea for *me* to be there. You obviously have stuff to sort out between yourselves, and—"

"Please," Vanessa interrupted him. "Please, Francesco." Then, after a long silence, she added: "Do it for me. Meet him at the agreed time, and don't tell him I'm coming."

"But I…"

"It's very important. Please. You don't know how grateful I would be to you."

Francesco looked out of the window into the night sky. A round sliver of moon, framed by wispy clouds, was hanging low over the rooftops, brightening the great expanse of the city below. He drew imaginary lines between the few visible stars, almost hoping that some direction could be offered to his steps, to his future. But the constellations were mute, and the path ahead of him, out in the wide world, still uncertain, inscrutable.

9

Paris

THE PARIS MORNING was rich with the aroma of strong
coffee and croissants. The first thing Francesco did when
he left the Gare du Nord was to look for a modest hotel
in which he could rest and freshen up after another almost
sleepless night. His money was starting to run out again,
so it was a while before he could find something within his
price range.

In the end he settled on a bed-and-breakfast off Rue du Fau-
bourg-Saint-Denis. As he crept up to his room, he was surprised
to hear gusts of alcoholic laughter still wafting down the corridors and to see hulking men in boxer shorts and out-of-season
St Patrick's Day hats roaming around with buckets in search of
an improbable ice dispenser, giving him the thumbs-up sign.

He slept for two hours, then grabbed a sandwich and set off
through the sun-filled streets of Paris. After a saunter round
the base of the Eiffel Tower and a lightning tour of the Louvre
and the Musée d'Orsay, he headed east towards Père Lachaise.

At the side entrance on Boulevard de Ménilmontant there was a bearded man selling odds and ends, including a detailed map of the place. A flight of irregular steps took him up to one of the western avenues of the cemetery, which at that time looked deserted. Since he was early for his meeting with Pierre, he decided to take a look around at some of the tombs.

Oscar Wilde's grave, with its emasculated harpy-like Sphinx and dingy marble covered in lipstick, was an ironic monument to someone who had preached the ideal of beauty to an entire generation of aesthetes. Francesco fancied he could see a familiar figure in a black tailcoat, with top hat, cigar and a lily in his buttonhole, leaning in a languid pose against that grey, soulless parallelepiped and drawling in a lordly tone:

"Only those who know they are not immortal are frightened of death. And only those who know they are mortal are frightened of eternity."

He continued to stroll around for a while. He had just walked past Sarah Bernhardt's tomb, and was making his way towards those of Molière and La Fontaine, when he glanced at his watch and realized that he had forgotten to turn the hands forward by an hour after crossing the Channel. His appointment was in less than ten minutes' time.

Disorientated, he went down a long, cobbled avenue at a brisk pace. Every so often he halted at a crossroads, turning the map in his hands as he tried to get his bearings in that maze.

"If that one's Delacroix's tomb," he said to himself, "I need to go left at the next turn, then right, then left again…"

And he broke into a half-run among narrow lanes lined with gravestones, obelisks, statues, vaults and sepulchres, all enveloped in heady sunshine, broken at times by the sweet-scented shade of trees.

In the end he did reach the tomb of Chopin, which was situated in a quieter and more secluded part of the cemetery. It was a rather modest monument, but was gracefully done and decorated with fresh flowers. Pierre had not arrived, so he took shelter from the sun and sat down on a stone step along the margin of the footpath, just opposite the Polish composer's grave.

Ten, fifteen, twenty minutes passed, and no one turned up, except for the odd tourist or visitor who stopped for a moment to take a photo and then moved on. Restless, Francesco got to his feet and began to explore the surrounding burial places, and as he climbed up a little alleyway at the back of Chopin's tomb, he stumbled across the graves of Luigi Cherubini and Vincenzo Bellini. With only a bunch of shrivelled flowers and a dry wreath at their feet, they looked bare, untended, unloved.

As he turned back into Chemin Denon, he caught sight of a slender woman dressed in black, wearing sunglasses and with her hair tied back, walking with two men.

"Vanessa," he said, going up to her.

"Francesco."

Her companions were bulky individuals who looked uncomfortable in their white shirts and lounge suits. The fatter one was pouring with sweat.

"He didn't come?" Vanessa asked with a pained smile. Before Francesco could say anything, she added: "I knew it."

"Shall we wait a bit longer?"

"It's pointless. Let's take a walk."

They started to wander along the empty footpaths and avenues, with the two men in suits following a few yards behind. Vanessa kept silent, as if afraid of eavesdroppers among the deaf stones of the cemetery. Then, as they circled a lawned roundabout with a tall monument at its centre, she said:

"I think I owe you some explanations."

They sat on a bench under the shadow of a tall tree. She unclasped her hair and shook it loose on her shoulders, then lifted her glasses above her head and turned to look Francesco in the eyes.

"Pierre is a serial con man," she said.

Francesco raised an eyebrow.

"He spends his life defrauding people of vast amounts of money," she continued. "He uses various aliases in different countries. I'm only his latest victim."

There was a long silence. It was obvious that she was not able to say more unless prompted to do so. Her two minders were sitting on another bench nearby, smoking cigarettes.

"Aren't you his wife?" Francesco asked.

After a pause she said: "I'm not the only one to enjoy that privilege."

"I'm not sure I follow."

"He's married to many women."

"At the same time?"

She nodded. "Just to swindle them out of their fortunes. He's been married for years to an Italian lady called Gabriella and a Dutch woman called Linda."

"Was the parcel meant for her?"

"For her and the Dutch police."

"Can I ask you what was in it?"

"Just some photos to reassure them about Pierre's good health. They thought he was dead."

"Do you know what happened to the package?"

"I have no idea. My best guess is that Pierre got wind of it and asked some thug to take it from you."

"Was it the Dutch woman, Linda, who called the ambulance?"

Vanessa nodded. "I think I need a smoke."

She waved at one of the men in suits, who came over, tapped a cigarette out of the packet and gave her a light before returning to his bench. As he did so, Francesco studied his head and wondered, for a moment, if this could be the same man he had seen on tape running down the stairs after the mysterious incident in the Slotermeer building.

"Pierre's destroyed my life," she went on, taking a long pull and exhaling. "I met him around two years ago at one of my exhibitions. We started to see each other and got married a few months later in Venice. I never knew for sure what he did for a living. He told me he owned some plastics factories in China and Hong Kong, and that he was going to sell them and reinvest some of the proceeds in modern art or the stock market. I had no reason to think he was lying: he always carried a lot of money in his pockets and took me to the best hotels and restaurants – bought me wonderful gifts." She took another deep draw on her cigarette. "What I didn't know is that he'd set his sights on the trust my father had created for me. He convinced me that it could benefit from his expertise in finance and investment, and I was so foolish that I let him be appointed as one of the trustees." There was another pause. "He started buying prints, paintings and sculptures from foreign art dealers and then sold them back to the trust at an overinflated price.

The oldest trick in the book. In a short time, he has embezzled millions of marks."

"No one tried to stop him?" Francesco said.

"This only came out a few weeks ago, during an internal audit of the trust. At first we were not sure about the real scale of the fraud. He's been diverting the payments into a complex network of bank accounts. So I employed an international private-investigation agency" – she gestured towards the two men – "and discovered that he was involved in similar scams in other countries, under a number of identities. In Holland he's wanted for a life-insurance fraud, in Spain for some kind of Ponzi or pyramid scheme, in Belgium for false invoicing and money laundering… And these are only some of the crimes we know about: every day new details emerge." She extinguished the cigarette against the iron frame of the bench, then threw it into a bin.

"So, hang on – you want him arrested?" Francesco asked.

"I just want him out of my life," Vanessa said, with a rigid expression. "What I *don't* want is a scandal. I cannot afford it. It would ruin my reputation. I'm not interested in getting the money back: all I'm asking for is a divorce."

"He won't agree to that?"

For the first time, the hint of a smile crept over her face.

"You don't know how greedy and vindictive he is. When he found out that his accounts had been frozen and he'd been removed from the board of trustees, he began to threaten me. He said: 'If you don't give me half of all your money and properties, I'll drag you through the mud.'"

"So what are you going to do now?"

"I want to offer him an easy way out." She got to her feet. "Shall we go?"

They started to walk in silence down a cobbled avenue, with
the two investigators in tow. At the bend of the road, Vanessa
stopped and went over to a monumental tomb that rose on the
left, a small temple supported by slender Corinthian columns
and surrounded by a rusty iron railing. Under its stone roof were
two figures: a man and a woman lying there next to each other.
Their blackened statues, eroded by time, were a grim reminder
of the transient nature of all earthly passions and affairs.

"This must be the grave of Héloïse and Abelard," Francesco
said, coming up behind her with the map.

Vanessa nodded and peered past the railings.

"*Treu bis zum Tod*," she muttered. Then, after a long pause,
she turned to Francesco and said: "Will you help me?"

"Help you? To be honest, I'd rather not be involved, Vanessa.
I can't see how I come into all this. I've got my own life and
my own little problems to sort out."

"But you must help me, Francesco. He seems to have taken
to you so well – I'm sure he'll listen to you. And I'll compensate
you for the trouble."

"I'm sorry. I don't want any money."

"We know he's going to be in Rome for a book launch on
Wednesday evening, at the Libreria del Corso. All I'm asking
you to do is to give him this letter" – she produced a small envelope from her crocodile-skin handbag – "and tell him that
this is my final offer. Can you do that for me?"

There followed a tense pause, broken only by the singsong
chirr of the crickets. In the end, with a tentative gesture and a
half-smile, Francesco took the letter from Vanessa.

"I just hope I won't get another knock on my head for my
services," he said.

"Tell him this is his last chance," said Vanessa. She slid down her glasses and added ambiguously: "If he doesn't accept, then he'll leave me no choice." The delicate wrinkle that Francesco had seen furrowing her brow that night in Cologne had reappeared once more.

As they left the cemetery, Vanessa asked him to write his details down on a piece of paper, and said she'd be in touch over the next few days.

"Just promise me," she said, as she got into a black car driven by one of her minders, "that you'll let me know straight away what he says... Thank you." She closed the door and, as the car pulled away, her face, without turning once, tautened into a mournful expression.

Now that he was alone again, Francesco started to reflect on what he should do next. The metro station was only a few minutes' walk away. From there he could get to the Gare de Lyon and then take the first train to Turin or Milan. All being well, the next morning he would be back in Italy and could draw a line under this whole mess, resuming his uncomplicated life as a university student.

"Beeep... beeep... beeep..."

Francesco wheeled round: a car horn was blaring behind him. He could not see where the noise was coming from, so he continued to walk towards the metro station.

"Beeeep... beeeep..."

On the other side of the street, beyond a cloud of smoke from a passing van, a red sports car appeared, and a face whose Levantine features Francesco recognized all too well stuck itself out of the window and shouted:

"Hey, handsome! How much do you charge?"

"Bloody hell…" Francesco whispered.

There was a dangerous reverse manoeuvre, a reckless three-point turn across a junction, a screeching of tyres, a hooting of the horn, an echoing volley of imprecations in French, and there he was – that living, breathing phenomenon – climbing out of his car in one slithering movement and standing in front of Francesco.

"Sorry I'm a bit late," he said with a grin, staring at Francesco from behind his sunglasses. "Nasty traffic around here."

"Even on a Sunday?"

"Even on Sunday. No place to park. Horrible."

"You all right?"

"Yeah, I'm all right. I'm always all right."

"All sorted?"

"What?"

"Your pecuniary impasse."

"Yeah, all under control, for the time being. I think the two of us need to have a little chinwag, eh?"

"Why?"

"Why not? Come on, get into the car."

"What?"

"Get – in – the – car. What's the matter, gone deaf?"

Francesco climbed into the passenger's seat.

"Buckle up," Pierre said, closing the door.

And with these words, he shot off.

"Where are we going?" Francesco tried to ask.

"We're going on a bear hunt. We're going to catch a big one…"

"Seriously, Pierre, where are we off to? I was intending to start heading back to Italy…"

"No problem, man… No problemo… I'll take you back to base. I'm going the same way."

"I can go by train."

"You'll get there much faster if you come with me." As the car stopped at a traffic light, Pierre revved up a few times, and the engine let out raucous growls. "Hear the sound of music? Six cylinders – six gas-guzzling babies suckling away. Just sit back and relax, Francesco – re-*lax*: let the beast take you home."

"I've just met with Vanessa," Francesco announced in a flat voice.

An imperceptible grimace stole up the corner of Pierre's mouth. "I know."

"You know?"

"I followed your little tryst from a distance. I didn't want to intrude."

"Look, Pierre, I've been dragged into this against my own will. I want nothing to do with it. Here's the letter Vanessa's asked me to give you."

"What is it?"

"I haven't a clue. She says it's her final offer."

"Mm… now you got my attention."

Without stopping the car, he took the envelope from Francesco and ripped it open. He pulled out what looked like a cheque, had a quick look at it and put it back inside.

"Is that all she can afford?"

Francesco shrugged. "She said it was your last opportunity."

"My last opportunity?"

"To come out unscathed."

"Oh, I see. So she's threatening me now? What is she going to do? Get Interpol to issue a Red Notice? She'll have to add at least two zeroes to this if she wants to do business with me. Has she forgotten how much she's worth?"

He took out a lighter from his pocket and set fire to one corner of the envelope. When it was half burnt, he slowed the car down and eased it out of the window.

"That's the smell of money burning," he said.

A few minutes later, they were belting down the Autoroute du Soleil at 200 kilometres per hour.

"What's the speed limit in France?" Francesco asked.

"Ad lib."

"Seriously?"

"I think that driving under a hundred and thirty is a criminal offence."

"I see. And remind me, how fast do you have to go to break the sound barrier?"

"Why, do you think we're going too fast? We're just cruising. See that little hand there? That one. It's not even on 4,000 revs… At this speed, I can drive with my eyes closed and just one finger on the wheel."

"Well, don't do that before I receive my last rites."

They continued to hurtle along in silence for a while. Just as they were going past the exit for Auxerre, Pierre switched on the radio, lit up a cigarette and asked in a casual tone: "So, what else did Vanessa tell you?"

Francesco looked out of the window.

"I don't really want to talk about it, if it's OK."

"Come on, don't be shy. We're friends now, right?"

Francesco remained silent for a while, then turned to look at Pierre.

"You want to know what she told me?"

"Go on, surprise me."

Francesco turned again to look out of the window.

"I dunno. She was talking about some… situations."

"Situations."

"In various countries. Something about embezzled money, bigamy, life-insurance fraud… that sort of thing."

"Fraud? Is that the word she used? 'Fraud'?"

"I think so."

There was a long pause, then Pierre burst out laughing.

"Wahahahahaha!"

"What's so funny?"

"Wahahahahaha!"

He slapped the steering wheel several times and couldn't stop his hoarse guffaws of laughter. A tear was just about to spill from his right eye.

"Fraud…" He shook his head, becoming suddenly serious. "Fraud… There's many sides to each story, you know. The truth is like a roll of the dice: the more you shake them, the more numbers you get. You ask ten different people about something they've seen, and you'll get ten different versions… Do you want to know how things really stand? Listen to this, and then you tell *me* who's the fraud, all right?"

"All right."

Pierre flicked the ash from his cigarette.

"One evening – it must've been around three years ago – I was with this woman, Linda. We were coming back from a party at some friends', and we were a bit squiffy, if you know what I mean. Anyway, after another glass or two, we got undressed and went to bed, and when the lights went off we started talking about this and that – you know – life after death,

God, the angels… the whole shebang. So, I was almost falling asleep when I got a kind of itch on my neck. I started feeling around and noticed a little lump under the skin, here, on this side. Feel it, go on…"

"Keep your eyes on the game, man."

"Don't worry, Francesco, relax. Didn't I tell you? I'm in cahoots with death. Go on, have a little touch."

Francesco stretched out his hand and detected a small swelling under Pierre's left ear. When Pierre was satisfied that Francesco had felt it, he turned his eyes back to the road and resumed his story.

"Now, it's one thing to talk in the abstract about death and eternity, about the Man in the Sky and the Four Horsemen of the Apocalypse, and it's quite another thing to find yourself up against a lump on the neck in the middle of the night – you get my meaning? I said to myself, 'Well, bugger me sideways, it's the end of the road.' You live a quiet life, you get up every morning, eat, drink, sleep and da-daah! There's a lump sprouting on your neck and before you know it you're a goner… The point is, I shat myself."

"Did you tell Linda?"

"Course not, she was fast asleep by then. And when you're asleep you don't want to hear about other people's existential quandaries."

"Fair point."

"So the next morning I go to see a friend of mine, a doctor, a specialist. He takes a look at me, pokes and prods the spot and says, 'It's just a benign cyst, nothing to worry about.' So I run to the nearest church and light a candle to holy St Declan, who saved my bacon, and then I rush over to Linda's office to take her out and celebrate. When I get there, I call her from reception and she says, 'Sorry, Pierre, but I have a lunch meeting with one of the partners. Maybe we can go out for a pizza tonight?'"

He took the last drag from his cigarette and threw it out of the window in disgust.

"So in the morning I was thinking I'd better mug up on *The Tibetan Book of the Dead*, and now she's telling me to piss off? A meeting with one of the partners, eh? Right. Anyway, that's when the idea of a little practical joke popped into my head. That evening she found me in bed with a thermometer in my mouth. 'What's wrong with you, Pierre?' she says. 'You're looking off-colour tonight…' 'It's nothing, dear,' I tell her, 'don't worry.' She goes: 'You sure? You're really pale. You should see the doctor tomorrow.' I say: 'Actually I have been to the doctor today – that's why I came to your office.' 'Oh yeah? And what did he say?' 'He says that if I'm lucky I've got maybe another two or three years.' And I made her feel the lump under my ear."

"That was cruel."

"Cruel? Nah, just an innocent prank – the kind you get in Boccaccio. Well, I'll leave you to imagine the sobbing, the crying, the scenes of hysteria. Let's get to *el nitto-gritto*. So I pretend to go through more tests and examinations – incidentally, she never offered to come with me, too busy at work – and a few weeks later I take her to one side and with a cadaver's face I tell her, 'Linda, I've been thinking it over. I don't want to leave you without a penny.' 'What do you mean?' she says. 'Just look after yourself and try to get better. Don't worry about me.' 'No, Linda, I *am* worried about you, really worried. That's why I think it would be a good idea if we take out proper life insurance.' 'What are you talking about?' she says. "No one's gonna give you life insurance in these conditions.' 'You know what they say where I live? What the eye sees not, the wallet rues not.' And I told her my doctor friend would be happy to oblige if someone asked me to have a medical."

"That sounds faintly illicit."

"That's what she said too, but I explained that it was all in a good cause. With the insurance payment she could buy something nice – I don't know, a flat in the Jordaan or a house on the Côte d'Azur, for example. That's a good cause, isn't it? Anyway, to cut a long story short, I managed to persuade her. It should also be said, for the record, that Linda was already rolling in it."

"Rolling in it?"

"Both old and new mint. You know what old thingummy used to say?"

"Who?"

"The one with the beard and the long hair. The one who brought peace and harmony to all the peoples of the world."

"Jesus?"

"No, no, the other guy, same face... old doodad... The Beatles... what's his name?"

"John Lennon?"

A stinging slap landed on Francesco's thigh.

"Good man! What did he say? 'All you need is...'"

"Love."

"Yeah – love my arse. The world is a shit hole, Francesco – a she-*it* hole. Anyway, a few months pass and my condition starts to get worse – all a put-up job, of course. So I tell Linda: 'It's a shame you have to pay all that money in tax on the insurance.' 'Don't worry, darling,' she says, 'it doesn't matter.' 'Sure, but maybe with that money you could buy something nice – I don't know, a new car or a diamond bracelet for instance.' 'What are you proposing to do?' 'Well, maybe we can put the money into a charity, some sort of neck-tumour trust. That way we won't have to pay tax.' 'But are you sure it's legal, Pierre?' 'Of course it's legal, and it's all in a good cause. Nobody will notice, and we're not gonna hurt anyone.' So a few weeks later, once I'd made my will, I take her to one side again and tell her: 'Linda, you know this charitable organization for cancer research?' 'Yes?' 'Well, I've been thinking. It's a shame to leave it like that, dormant… Why don't we organize a big fund-raising party and invite all your lawyer friends?' 'But isn't that illegal, Pierre?' 'Come on, you studied law. You know there's illegal and illegal.' Then, of course, I started to enjoy the situation and began trundling around in a wheelchair and all that kind of stuff. But it was just a joke, a harmless hoax. So who's the real fake here? Tell me. Who's the real *fraud*?" And he broke into uproarious laughter.

"How did the endgame pan out?" Francesco asked.

"Well," Pierre said, heading off a coughing fit, "when things got out of control, I did a Reggie Perrin – an Arthur Cravan."

"You what?"

"I pulled a disappearing act. Just another bit of Dada, you know? My only mistake was to pocket the insurance money and dissolve the trust too quickly. I should have carried on the prank a bit longer. But I'd started to lose interest: I'd realized that it was time to be off to fresh woods and pastures new."

At the next petrol station, they stopped to refuel and got out to stretch their legs. Pierre smoked a nervous cigarette and made a series of calls from a phone box, while Francesco sat on a sunny patch of lawn, thinking about Chloe and Kyle, and the imminent end of his InterRail trip. After ten minutes or so, they were once again in a red projectile tearing down the fast lane of the French motorway, heading south.

"How do you tilt the seats back inside this spaceship?" Francesco asked, once they had reached cruising speed.

"Why? Do you want to sleep?"

"No, I'd just like to close my eyes."

"You're not curious to hear about Vanessa?"

"I think I'll pass, if it's all right. Another time. Do we have to keep going at 200 kph?"

"Does the name Schreiter remind you of anything?"

Francesco sighed and shook his head.

"Have you heard of Himmler?"

"You mean Hitler's right-hand man?"

"That's the one. Well, Erich Schreiter, Vanessa's grandfather, was Himmler's accountant – what we would call today his 'personal financial advisor'. Do you remember when I told you that modern society is a big chicken run? Himmler had already figured it out over sixty years ago. He was a precocious genius. When he was young, he set up a chicken farm and—"

"You're pulling my leg."

"It's true. I swear, it's all true, you can check it out in the history books. The trouble is that his chicken-rearing business was a total disaster, so he had to look for another job. But since he was a smart guy, he went into politics straight away, and worked his way up through the ranks. A few years later, he goes to the big chief in person and says to him, 'Why don't we set up a concentration camp, like the English? I have a bit of experience, you know. We can bung in all the Jews, Poles, poofters, commies – even the Chinks if we get a chance. It's a doddle.' 'All right,' says Hitler, 'but what's in it for us?' That's when a little fellow, Vanessa's granddad, pops up and says: 'Well, out of every stiff we get a few gold teeth – say twenty Deutschmarks, for example – one pair of shoes, three marks, a watch, another ten marks… and then there's all the silverware, jewels, furniture, paintings, houses and bank accounts they leave behind, which we can confiscate.' 'Hmm…' says Hitler, 'not a bad idea… well done, Himmler, I'll give you a medal.'"

"What's this got to do with Vanessa?"

"If you just let me finish, you'll find out. So after the big success with the concentration camps, Grandpa Schreiter says to Himmler, 'Listen, Heinrich, we've built a chicken run for the extermination of the Jews, but perhaps we should also set up a farm and rear some chicks for the advancement of the Aryan race, what do you think?' That's how Himmler came up with the idea for the *Lebensborn* programme."

"*Lebensborn?*"

"Yeah, they decided to build some factories – or *fuck*tories I should say – for the procreation of the perfect German breed. They picked up the most beautiful girls with blue eyes and blond hair and mated them with SS soldiers. What's that face?"

"You're making it all up."

"No I'm not. I swear on my mother's kidneys, it's all written down in the annals of history. So anyway, that's where Arthur Schreiter, Vanessa's father, was conceived. You see? We're getting warmer. Then things started to turn brown-coloured for the Nazis, as you know, and Herr Hitlerstache put a bullet through his own *Kopf*. Himmler went out too, not with a bang but a whimper, but good old Schreiter managed to sneak away to Switzerland. It's not easy to bump off an accountant, you see, especially a German one. So Schreiter moves all his operations to Zurich with his son Arthur. An honest bunch of people, the Swiss, though they like to keep quiet about the way they make money. I bet they'd be on the beggars' list if all the cash and gold held in their vaults went back to the countries of origin."

Pierre lit up another cigarette and opened the window a crack.

"So years go by," he continued, "people forget, and Schreiter junior, Arthur, begins to make a new life for himself – not too difficult with all the millions his father's stashed away. But blood's thicker than water, so he makes sure that Papa's savings are put to good use – and when he's twenty-five, he buries his dad on the quiet, grows himself a toothbrush moustache and goes back to Germany. As soon as he gets there he changes his name from Schreiter to Schreiber – just in case – then marries a respectable German woman with blond hair and blue eyes, buys fine art, makes charitable donations and sets up a company to trade with developing countries – bazookas, machine guns, grenades, landmines, bombs – all perfectly legit. Then, of course, he sends his kids to the smartest schools, gets them the best piano teachers and so on and so forth… In short, he recycles dirty old money through fresh young blood. Do you understand now why our friend wants to avoid any scandal or publicity?"

"So you're saying that Vanessa's the daughter of an arms trafficker and the granddaughter of a Nazi officer? The same Vanessa who's written *Art and Revolution*?"

"Let me tell you something: where there's a radical thinker, where there's a left-wing artist, there's usually old money underpinning them – old money that is taken for granted and rarely questioned. *Pecunia non olet*. How do they put it in Rome? *Er più pulito c'ha la rogna*. The cleanest have scabs all over."

"Unbelievable."

"That's what I'm saying. So do you think it's fair that a little bint like her, who's been splashing around in a sea of loot tainted with human blood, can come up to me and tell me I'm a *fraud*? If the money that jangles in her pocket could talk, if it could start to howl, I don't think she'd be able even to face her own reflection in a mirror – her and those Oneiric bullshit paintings of hers."

Pierre narrowed his eyes and remained silent for a few moments, as their car continued to spin along in the fast lane overtaking other vehicles which seemed stationary in comparison.

"And the wonderful thing," he went on, taking a long pull from his cigarette, "is that the law keeps hassling guys like me – guys like me who'd never hurt a fly and just want to be left alone... The law never dreams of going after the real criminals... You see, Francesco, as we speak, all around us, everywhere," and with a sweep of his hand he seemed to indicate the whole world, "people are robbing, murdering, buggering and betraying each other for all they're worth... but since they do so with a smile on their lips, nobody ever says a thing... instead, they come and bust my balls. Now let me tell you another story, a true story, just a short one – it happened only last month. Remember fatso-face – you know – botox-brow, trout-lips, bowling-pin legs – the two-tonne-tit diva, the famous opera singer? Well, she was performing at a charity concert in some Asian country: all the money was supposed to go to the children of Ethiopia – oh yes, if wishes were horses...

So her agent draws up a really neat contract to get worldwide satellite coverage. Problem is, he doesn't manage to sell the programme to any of the big American networks, and he ends up with a tidy sum to pay. So what's he do? With the takings from the ticket sales he pays the soprano's fee, the organizers' expenses, the special effects, advertising, royalties, etc. etc. And he doesn't forget – why would he? – to cover the costs of his failed TV-rights deal. What do the children of Ethiopia get? Feck-all, as the Irish say. Minus tax and agent's commission, of course. See what I'm getting at? Everyone's at it: tax evasion, criminal bankruptcy, benefit scams, insider trading, forgery, bribe-taking, larceny, prostitution, child-trafficking, organ-trafficking – not to mention the dark dealings of big corporations, politicians, governments, the war crimes... But what do they do? They come and bust *my* balls." After a short pause he added: "You're not taking sides with lawyers or insurance people, are you?"

"I'm not taking sides with anybody," Francesco said.

Pierre jammed the gas pedal to the floor, switched off the radio and became silent for the rest of the journey.

10

Monte Carlo

IT WAS AROUND TEN O'CLOCK when Francesco emerged from a jittery slumber and realized that they were no longer on the motorway but winding their way down the narrow streets of the French Riviera.

"Ten kilometres to Monte Carlo?" he croaked, lifting up the seat back and yawning.

"Do you always sleep?" said Pierre.

"Are we stopping here?"

"I have a little business to do with a friend of mine, then we can go to the casino for a couple of punts."

"Who's this friend of yours?"

"A Russian fellow – Lithuanian, actually."

"Does he know you're going to see him?"

"Of course. I called his secretary earlier. He's not the sort of guy you can go and see without arranging a meeting beforehand. He's a busy man. Once I had to jump on a train to meet him in the first-class compartment between one stop and the next."

"What does he do?"

"Not sure. Asbestos, I think. I've never enquired. He's not the sort of guy you want to ask that kind of question."

They parked near the Port d'Hercule marina and strolled down to the docks. They stopped in front of the most luxurious boat moored in the harbour, a brand-new thirty-metre yacht with a futuristic design. It looked as if there was a party going on, and music and laughter could be heard from the upper deck. With a confident stride, Pierre approached the dimly lit gangplank, which was guarded by a craggy-looking, dark-suited individual around six foot nine in height and twenty stone in weight. Pierre raised his arm to touch fists with the guard.

"How'ya doing man?"

The guard neither blinked nor moved. Pierre put his arm down.

"*Chto?*" the guard said.

"Aren't you letting us in?"

"No."

"I'm here to see Mr Glinskis. I'm a friend of his. You don't recognize me?"

"No."

Pierre was losing his cool.

"Come on, man, I've driven six hundred miles to be here. I called earlier – he's expecting me."

The security guard mumbled something in his walkie-talkie. A reply buzzed through and he said:

"Mr Glinskis busy."

"What're you talking about? I have an appointment with him."

"Mr Glinskis busy." There was a threatening note in the man's voice.

"Does he know I'm here?"

"*Da*."

"And he won't see me?"

"Mr Glinskis busy."

"OK, so shall I come back tomorrow?"

The man mumbled again in his walkie-talkie and waited for a reply.

"*Nyet*. Not tomorrow."

"When, then?"

"Next year."

"Next year?" Pierre scoffed.

"*Konyechno*. If Mr Glinskis not busy."

Pierre made a half-step forward, as if he intended to confront the guard and edge past him.

"Come on, Pierre, let's go," whispered Francesco, holding his arm. "You don't wanna mess around with this guy – have you seen his face?"

"Yeah – a Christmas present from Easter Island."

"I've never seen so many storms brewing in one place."

"All right," Pierre hissed, jerking his head and turning to go. "All right. Bloody Russky."

"Perhaps he really is busy."

"Doesn't matter. I'll catch up with him some other time. Fancy a game of roulette?"

On the way to the casino, they stopped to pick up a black jacket and a crumpled pink tie for Francesco from Pierre's suitcase.

"Listen carefully," Pierre said, closing the boot of the car. "Just play red and black, odd and even, *passe* and *manque*, OK? Don't get too hot under the collar."

"I'll just watch."

"Oh yes, you'll just watch. I know your type, slyboots. Gently does it, all right? Don't get carried away."

On the short flight of stairs to the main entrance they met smiling couples going in and gloomy-faced gamesters going out. After Pierre bought the admission tickets and got some tokens from the chip counter, they parted in the main hall. Pierre went straight to the roulettes, where crowds of people were jostling and stretching to place their bets, while Francesco strolled about in the adjoining rooms, stopping for a while to observe the slot machines and the blackjack tables.

"I swear to God," said a short man of Spanish appearance in a worn-out suit, "I swear to God that if the dealer now pulls out an ace again, I'll eat this hundred-franc note, see?"

"*Vingt-et-un*," the dealer shouted.

"Pass him some salt," someone whispered behind Francesco.

When he went back to look for his friend, Francesco saw Pierre sitting at the high-stakes roulette table. A tall blonde girl was standing to his left and a red-haired woman to his right. He was winking, joking, laughing and gesticulating as he moved his chips around the green board to place his wagers or gather his winnings. Around him, people betrayed their personalities with their expressions and gestures. A skinny hand making a tentative foray into the betting area belonged to a sombrely dressed middle-aged lady with an austere face and a rigid grimace imprinted on her features. A coquettish brunette with a conspicuous cleavage pushed tokens every which way without a care in the world, drinking champagne and giggling in the ear of her sugar daddy. An impassive gentleman, perhaps an advantage player, kept darting his eyes around the table, betting every other turn and jotting down all the results in a tiny notepad.

Pierre had amassed mountains of chips in front of him, and was using both hands to place new bets. Francesco walked round to him.

"How are you doing?"

"Sensationally. You're not playing?"

"Just observing at the moment. Learning."

"Thirsty? Hungry?"

"Not really."

"You sure? Can I interest you in some *fiches* and chips?" Pierre tilted his head towards his tokens. "Try your luck."

"I'm unlucky at gambling."

"Come on, have a quick flutter. Take this and show me what you can do."

He put a hundred-franc chip in Francesco's hand.

Francesco continued to wander around from one room to the other, and stopped again at the blackjack tables, where a pot-bellied fellow – a professional gambler by the look of it – had caught his eye. He was dressed all in white, including his waistcoat and shoes, and was wearing a panama hat, a solid-gold watch and a long black beard. His tactics were somewhat rudimentary: they consisted in walking from one table to the other at an even pace and placing five hundred francs on every card that was being played. His colossal figure bobbed up and down behind the backs of the other players, and as the cards were laid down he moved on. Most of the time, the dealer won. The man, without batting an eyelid, took some more chips from his pockets and carried on with his awkward dance between the tables. In less than half an hour, Francesco watched him lose over a hundred thousand francs.

He returned to the roulette room, and for some time he stood at the far corner of a small-stakes table, watching the mindless obstinacy of the players with a certain sense of detachment. It occurred to him that this was a perfect image of our unfair society: some people win, others lose, money changes hands following the ups and downs of fortune. Then it starts all over again as new wagers are laid: some win, most lose, and the handy-dandy capers of money and fate strike up again. Pierre was right, in a way: this world is a shit hole.

One of the gamblers in front of him left, mumbling blasphemies and obscenities in Italian. Francesco sat down and waited until the croupier had paid the few winners and raked up the losing bets, before placing his hundred francs on red. He changed his mind and moved it across to black – and just before the ball started spinning he pushed it back into the reds' rectangle.

"*Rien ne va plus,*" the croupier announced.

The ball rolled as the wheel turned the opposite way, then both began to lose momentum and the ball started to bump and skip until it finally landed in one of the slots.

"*Seize – rouge, pair et manque.*"

The croupier put the prize money next to Francesco's bet and proceeded to clear the betting area.

Francesco stared at the table with an uncomprehending look. It seemed strange to him that his money could have doubled at the simple spin of a wheel. He hesitated, not knowing whether he was supposed to collect his win or not.

"*Mesdames et messieurs, faîtes vos jeux s'il vous plaît.*"

The ball started rolling again, and before Francesco could take his chips or place them somewhere else, the croupier declared that no further bets were allowed.

"*Vingt-trois – rouge, impair et passe.*"

The croupier nudged four hundred-franc tokens towards Francesco, who steered them to the blacks' area with an impulsive gesture, as if an external hand had pushed them.

A few instants later the croupier shouted:

"*Quatre – noir, pair et manque.*"

This time Francesco decided to hold back seven hundred francs, and was about to put one hundred on *passe* when, for a brief moment, he locked eyes with the croupier. It was then that he heard a voice inside telling him: "Put it on zero. All on zero." And so he did: he stretched across the table and placed eight hundred francs on the bank's number, among the puzzled looks of some of the other players.

"*Rien ne va plus.*"

The ball continued to spin and hop around the roulette for what seemed like minutes. Francesco closed his eyes, but he already knew the outcome: he could have waged his own life on that single result.

"*Zéro,*" said the croupier, with a slight gasp.

There were cries of surprise and animated comments as Francesco collected the prize money and left with almost twenty-nine thousand francs in tokens. He walked straight to the cashier and exchanged his chips for real notes, then went back to check on his friend.

Pierre's table was now half-deserted. Gone was the tall blonde girl, gone was the red-haired woman: sitting next to him was a very old lady dressed in black, bearing an uncanny resemblance to the widow he had met at Vanessa's party in Cologne. A few paltry chips were scattered in front of him, and he was visibly tipsy.

"Is that the smell of money burning?" Francesco said, taking his place by Pierre's side.

"It's a diabolical game," Pierre said. "Did you know that if you add all the numbers on the wheel you get 666, the number of the Beast?"

"What's happened? You were winning a packet."

"I know. I thought it was gonna be my night." He placed his last chips on black. "Just red and black, red and black, odd and even – that's the secret…"

"That's what Dostoevsky said the day he wagered his shirt and trousers."

The ball and the wheel started to spin in opposite directions.

"*Rien ne va plus*," said the croupier with a weary voice.

"Well, my friend," continued Pierre, putting a hand on Francesco's arm, his gaze still fixed on the ball, "if it lands on black, we can spend the night in a hotel, and if it's red… well, I guess we'll have to sleep in the car tonight. Since you can sleep anywhere, that won't be a problem for you."

The ball wobbled several times and seemed to be settling on the twenty-eight – a black – but one last bad-tempered flick of Fortune's finger made it tumble into the adjoining slot.

"*Sept – rouge, impair et manque.*"

"Holy *merde*!" hissed Pierre.

As they were coming out of the casino and walking towards the car, Pierre turned and made as if to go back inside.

"Do you still have those hundred-francs I gave you, by any chance? Or even fifty?"

"Let's go, Pierre…"

"That bloody redhead… it's her fault: she jinxed me."

"Let's go, Pierre."

"Come on, just a little game of *trente-et-quarante* and we'll be off. I think I've got quite a bit of loose change in my pockets."

Francesco finally managed to pull him back from the entry to the casino. It was almost two in the morning.

"Are hotels very expensive around here?" Francesco asked in a casual tone, as Pierre was starting to settle down on the seat for the night.

"What was that?" he said, rubbing his eyes and yawning.

"Let's see if we can find a good room. I'd kill for a shower."

"What are you talking about? We have no money. My cash machine, Mr Glinskis, will only see me next year."

"Why are you worrying about money all of a sudden? Didn't you say that intelligent animals don't need it?"

"Uh?" Pierre darted a questioning glance, first at Francesco's face and then at his right hand, which was clutching a folded wad of banknotes.

"Come on, it's starting to get cold," Francesco said. "This one's on me." And he did an impression of Pierre's piratical wink.

Once, just once, he had succeeded in taking the monarch of make-believe, the sultan of surprise, by surprise.

11

Rome, Genzano

ALL ROADS LEAD TO ROME – at least, that's what Francesco had always been told. So the following morning, as if to prove this point, he insisted on taking charge of Pierre's car and headed first east and then south without checking any maps or taking much notice of the road signs. As Pierre lolled in the passenger seat with his sunglasses on, Francesco drove at a mere 110 km an hour, which on the Italian *autostrada* is close to standing still. And as they cruised down big-footed Italy past more or less familiar cities, Francesco had the impression that he was slipping down a large funnel, as if all the roads he had travelled on – in Germany, Sweden, Denmark, Holland, England, France – really did lead there, to the Eternal City, to his home.

They stopped to tank up and get a snack at a petrol station between Lucca and Prato. Pierre was in a terrible mood, and spent most of the time in a phone box with a cigarette in his hand and the receiver cradled between his shoulder and ear, often shouting and banging on the glass walls.

"Bitch," he said, stepping out of the phone box and flicking away the semi-burnt filter. "I'll show her who wears the trousers here. Let's go."

They continued to drive in silence through expansive green fields and gentle hills, often surmounted by medieval towns and castles, until Pierre turned his head to one side and dozed off. When he woke up it was almost five in the afternoon.

"Where are we?" he said, taking off his sunglasses and stretching.

"Near Orte…"

"Orte? So we're already there…" And he leant back in his seat, yawning as he shut his eyes again.

In fact they still had about fifty miles to go, and it was an hour later when they started to approach the city centre through an intricate tangle of roads, junctions, apartment blocks and traffic lights, with people crossing everywhere on foot and overtaking them left and right on *motorini* and Vespas. Pierre perked up and began to act as a co-pilot.

"Here you turn right… go left at the next turning… flick on the indicator… slow down here… you bloody jerk…"

The last remark wasn't addressed to Francesco, but to the driver next to them who – at a red light – was trying to overtake them by going up on the pavement on the right. The car was an old-model canary-yellow Fiat 500 Abarth with black ailerons and a stereo system fit to deafen a nightclub. The driver looked at them with dog-tired eyes, his hand dangling out of the window and tapping on the door to the music's rhythm, a toothpick sticking out of his bearded mouth. When, at the green, the man shot off and succeeded in his manoeuvre, Pierre shook his head in discontent.

"You're a timid driver. You're too respectful of others. We're in Rome here, not Geneva." He laid a hand on Francesco's shoulder and added: "Let me show you how people drive around here. The basic rule is the survival of the fittest."

Pierre slipped into the driving seat and showed Francesco "how people drove" in those parts, so that twenty minutes later they'd already reached the San Lorenzo district behind Stazione Termini.

"I'll be back in ten minutes, OK? I'll just drop off my bags and give you a lift home."

"Don't worry, the Laziali station is just round the corner."

"You sure? It's no trouble."

"Yes I'm sure. Trains are less dangerous, and I travel free."

"Well, do as you like. Listen, I've got this book launch on Wednesday, at the Libreria del Corso. You coming along? We can go for a drink or a bite in Trastevere after that."

"That'd be good. What time is the launch?"

"Six."

"OK."

They swapped addresses and telephone numbers and went their separate ways.

On the train to Albano, Francesco sat for most of the time in an empty compartment as the city outskirts glided past the window, anonymous and inexpressive: first the big tenement blocks of the Casilina district, then the ruins of Roman aqueducts, with clusters of shacks and lean-tos huddled around them behind the railway track, then the still-sunny greenery of the Campagna Romana, then drab Ciampino, followed by the cool lushness of the Alban Hills... The funnel continued to narrow.

Francesco closed his eyes and let himself be lulled by the gentle rocking of the train as it climbed round the slopes of Lake Albano and past the Pope's summer residence at Castel Gandolfo. He had gone from never having set foot outside Italy to travelling from one end of Europe to the other. It was time to return home. He was starting to feel tired: he needed to settle down and digest the impressions of the previous weeks – the new faces, events and sensations that were still whirling round in his head. He wanted to be reunited with the objects he was used to, look into familiar eyes, indulge in banal, habitual actions. In short, it was as if he was longing to embrace again the comfortable routine of his life.

When he stepped down off the local coach from Albano, Francesco drew a breath and gazed around him: he recognized the tree-lined road, the café with the same old men smoking outside, the steep downhill street – it all seemed to smile at him with a familiar nod.

He entered the gate to the council estate, descended the wide stone steps, walked under the window of Corradina, whose nineteen-year-old son Mariuccio was in prison for drug-dealing, went past Lenora's flat, from which emerged the cries of ancient *comari* playing *tombola*, and passed beneath Adriana's balcony, where her husband Enrichetto had been ambushed and killed with twenty-two stab wounds three months ago.

And then came the moment he'd been playing through his head a hundred times, just like the athlete who's getting ready for the long jump: he tests his footing, takes one short step forward and another one back, and then off he goes. Except that he knew he wouldn't be in for a soft landing. He hardly had time to ring the bell before the door opened and a shrill voice shouted in Genzanese dialect:

"Why didn't you call – even once?"

The words belonged to a housewife with a worn-out face and unkempt, fading red hair. A whiff of pan-fried anchovies and sautéed broccoli rabe came from the kitchen.

"Hi Mum."

"*Cammina, vié dentro*. I'm cooking dinner."

Francesco went in and closed the door behind him. The hall corridor was dark: the light of day had been sucked out of the farthest corners, and a wan mortuary glow from a bulb hanging from the ceiling lit his way to the kitchen. The table had been set only for two, but another place was quickly added.

"So, one month without any news," Francesco's mother said as she started cooking the pasta and Francesco sat at one end of the small table, near the window. "I thought you were dead or something. Travelling all alone…"

"I didn't exactly go into the Amazonian jungle."

"I know, but one month without a call, or even a postcard…" She didn't look at her son, but continued to stir the spaghetti in the boiling water.

"First of all it wasn't a month, but two and a half weeks – and secondly, I tried to call you once, but there was no answer."

His mother didn't comment, and kept busying herself around the cooker.

"I was thinking of staying over for the night. Would it be all right?"

"Of course."

"Marcella won't mind? Where is she?"

"Gone out with some friends."

A few minutes later, a plate of steaming-hot *spaghetti al pomodoro* was placed in front of Francesco.

"Eat, or it'll go cold," his mother said.

"What about Dad? Isn't he eating with us?"

A familiar noise – like the trumpeting of an old elephant – sounded in the direction of the toilet, and from its peeling white door emerged a big-bellied figure wearing a vest, with a cigarette in his mouth and a folded copy of *L'Unità* in his hand, three or four days' stubble on his chin, greasy hair, glasses all smudged up, the top two buttons of his trousers unfastened. That was his father.

"Ah! So Christopher Columbus is back, after five hundred years?"

"Hi, Dad," Francesco mumbled over his first mouthful of pasta.

"The Hero of the Two Worlds…"

"That was Garibaldi."

"You know what I mean."

"No, I don't."

"Do you think it's the right way to behave, staying out of touch all this time and not even giving your mother a ring?"

"I've already *told* Mum, I did try to call you once."

"Once?"

"I didn't have much time."

"But you did have time to go loafing around, eh?" Francesco's father took his place at the head of the table. "You only remember us when you need money or want to scrounge a meal, right?"

"Wrong. I haven't asked you for a penny in three years. How much is it for the food tonight?"

And they kept up their verbal guerrilla warfare over dinner, while Francesco's mother, hardly touching her plate, continued to scurry in submissive silence from the cooker to the sink and back.

"I think I'm going to have a lie-down," Francesco said rising to his feet, once fruit and coffee had been served. "I'm dead tired. *Buonanotte*."

Neither of his parents answered: their eyes were glued to the small black-and-white TV on the top of the fridge, which was showing a new episode of their favourite programme, *Derrick*.

"Didn't the Olympics start the other day?" Francesco tried again. "I think there's football on tonight – aren't Italy playing Poland?"

"Who cares," Sergio said, breaking his silence, "about twenty-two pampered idiots running around a pitch with a ball?"

"You used to like football. You took me to the stadium many times when I was a kid."

"I don't give a damn about anything any more. Now don't stand in front of the screen, will you?"

Francesco walked down the dark corridor and opened the door to his old room, that Black Hole of Calcutta in which he had spent his infancy and his teens, that familiar space with its accustomed things – the two beds, the pine-wood chest of drawers, the light-green wallpaper, Marcella's Duran Duran posters – in their usual place. A shiver of claustrophobia ran up his spine at the thought of his sister still leading a prisoner's life in that little den.

It was a warm evening, and the room smelt musty. To dissolve the knot of tension in his throat, Francesco jumped onto his bed and reached out to open the little window above to let in some fresh air. But the window refused to budge, so he climbed down off the bed dripping with sweat and overcome by an even more acute sense of suffocation.

There was a gentle knock at the door, and he went to open it.

"What's up, Mum?" he asked, leaning an elbow against the door frame.

"I'd forgotten... Zia Teresa cleaned your flat today and brought these over. They're for you."

And through the crack in the door came two coloured rectangles – a postcard and a letter.

"Thank you."

He closed the door and sat on his bed. The postcard was from Oxford: "Sorry I didn't come to London. Dan and I have decided to go on a three-month trip to Australia to sort ourselves out. The night you left he proposed to me. I'll always remember that evening in Lund. Sunny greetings and cloudy kisses, Kyle. PS: I still have your stuff here. I washed it, but the tomato stains haven't come off entirely – any time you want to pop by and collect it…"

The letter was from his Dutch rescuer, Boudewyn, and it included an invoice and some receipts. The hospital had sent in a bill for the ambulance and first aid, and he was just forwarding them on, together with his best wishes.

Francesco shook his head as he looked again at Kyle's postcard, and his mind started to wander. He was twenty-one years old, and all he had was a past and a shapeless future. He thought about Chloe, her gossamer blond hair, her fair skin, her soft brown eyes, and he dreamt of long years of intimacy together – a house in London, Paris or Rome, a life of travel, fulfilling work and profound cultural experiences – but then the sounds of his mother clanking pots in the kitchen and his father spitting phlegm into the toilet came through the walls, bringing home the reality of that little room in a nondescript council-estate flat on the outskirts of a small provincial town – and a sense of dissatisfaction and inadequacy tugged at him and made him come to.

He barged back into the kitchen, where the television was pouring out sounds and images into almost complete darkness. His father was sprawling in his chair, and if it hadn't been for the red glow of his fag end, Francesco would have said he was asleep. His mother was absorbed in the latest exciting crime case and somehow managed at the same time to do some crochet work.

"Is it OK if I make a quick call?" Francesco said.

"Ask your father. Sergio?" His mother turned her gaze for an instant from the white light, streaked by the cigarette smoke.

But Francesco's father, offended by their previous argument, just drained his umpteenth glass of Amaretto di Saronno – sucking the last drops out, removing the glass for a moment from his lips and then licking its sugary rim with the tip of his tongue – and ignored both his son's question and his wife's prod.

"Can I make a call, Dad?" Francesco ventured again, in conciliatory tones.

After a few more moments of silence, a hoarse voice rose from the far corner of the kitchen.

"Do as you like. Your father's authority means shit to you."

"Thanks."

"By the way," Sergio said, as his son was retreating down the corridor.

"Yes?"

"What's his name... Leonardo, your friend, the one with an earring... He called three or four times... He wanted to know when you were coming back."

"All right, cheers. I'll call him tomorrow."

Francesco went over to the phone and dialled Chloe's number. After a few rings, a girl's voice answered.

"Hello?"

"Chloe?"

"Yes?"

"It's Francesco here."

"Francesco. So good to hear from you. How are you?"

"I'm fine, I'm fine. I've just got back to Rome – Genzano, actually, my hometown. I thought I'd give you a ring and say hello, and..."

There was a longish pause.

"I'll be coming to Rome for the weekend," Chloe said.

"What? Really?"

"With my boyfriend."

"Oh."

"I'm joking."

"Right."

"With my boyfriend's mum, I meant."

"Oh."

"I'm joking."

"Look, Chloe" – Francesco cleared his throat – "maybe I haven't told you, but I have this heart condition..."

"Oh, I'm sorry."

"Yeah, especially with anything to do with you."

"What does that mean?"

"I suppose it means that I love you."

There was a longer pause.

"No one's said those words to me before."

"I've never said those words to anyone before."

"Well, I guess I'll see you soon, then."

"When are you coming, exactly? I can't wait."

"I'll be there on Thursday morning."

"Shall I meet you at the airport?"

"You wouldn't find me there."

"Why?"

"Because I'll be travelling by train. I'm leaving on Wednesday."

"Then I'll come and meet you at Termini. What time will you get there?"

"Hang on a sec, let me… Ten fifteen, it says here."

"OK, I'll be there."

"Look forward. Bye for now."

"Bye." He smacked a kiss into the receiver and hung up.

As he went back inside his old room Francesco whispered to himself: "Did I really say 'I love you' and kiss the phone?" His bad mood had all of a sudden evaporated. He lay on his bed and kicked his feet in the air, laughing, then picked up a volume of poetry belonging to his sister and began to leaf through it with listless hands, hardly reading the words. "All poetry is fake," he thought. "Love is not something you can commit to paper. You're lucky enough if you can feel it just once in your life." He snapped the book shut. "Mmm, this is material for good poetry. All I need is rhymes now." He switched off the light and tried to sleep, but his thoughts kept going back to Chloe and the idea of seeing her again soon. He smiled in the dark, then lifted his wrist and, looking at the phosphorescent hands of his watch, realized that it was getting on for midnight. The stifling heat and the exasperating wait for Marcella drove him out of the room. By now the television was off, but his father, who could rarely get off to sleep unless he knew everyone else was already in bed, sat ensconced on his kitchen chair in the near-darkness, listening to classic Romanesco songs on a local radio station and smoking an untipped cigarette. He looked inscrutable. Francesco quietly opened the kitchen window, pulled up a chair in front of him and sat down, then said:

"Anything new?"

"Yes. Italy's lost."

"Italy's lost?"

"Three-nil to Poland. Bunch of clowns. Got beaten by a team of window-cleaners. We're not even good at football any more. Pah."

"Any other news?"

"About what?"

"I don't know. About work?"

"Nah." Sergio drew from his cigarette. "They've just laid off more people at the steelworks. Another fifty souls put on slow roast." He coughed, and his eyes became slits of gloom.

"Have you accepted the redundancy payment?"

"Nope. The Union advised against it. They say if you accept you're out for good. There's still a small chance a German company takes over and re-employs some of us. You enjoyed your trip?"

"I did, yes. It was great."

"What did you see?"

And Francesco launched on an abridged version of his recent peregrinations, avoiding any mention of Pierre and unpleasant or embarrassing situations. To Sergio, who had never set foot outside Rome except for his military service in Apulia – from which he had got himself returned to sender by faking depression – who preferred the local wines to the most sought-after crus and champagnes, whose entire knowledge of the world was dependent on the TV's cataract-stricken eye, his son's narrative sounded like a fairy tale, especially at this late hour and in the haze of an alcoholic fug.

"Did you like what you saw there?" Sergio asked.

"I did. I did. And I wouldn't mind trying to live abroad for a while. In England or Holland, for example. Just to see what it's like."

"Hm, I wouldn't do that," Sergio said, getting to his feet with a theatrical swipe of the hand and stubbing the cigarette out in the ashtray. "Life's much better here. There's no place like home. What's the point of trotting off round the world? Wherever you go, it's the same: people eat, shit and sleep. What did poor old Gran say? *Quanno 'a formica vorze morì*—"

"*Misse l'ala*. Sure. When the ant decides to die, it grows wings. But maybe the place it flies to is better than the little hole it was living in."

"I doubt it." Sergio turned off the radio and licked out the dregs from the bottom of his glass, before adding: "Your sister's not back. I'm off to bed. Put the light out, OK?"

"I'm coming too."

But at that moment a faint, slow creak was heard from the front door. Sergio put his head out into the corridor, switched the light on and, tapping a non-existent watch on his wrist, said to his daughter: "What do you think this is, a bed-and-breakfast? You only come here to sleep, eh? It's nearly one o'clock. Who's working tomorrow morning?"

"It's half-past twelve," Marcella corrected him, "and tomorrow I'm on the afternoon shift. Hi, Francesco!" she then said, surprised to see her brother at the far end of the corridor. Francesco waved a hello to her.

Sergio's wife darted out of the bedroom.

"Don't shout, you'll wake the people downstairs—"

"Do you think it's right that your daughter comes back at this time of night?"

"Don't shout, they'll start banging."

"Well, do you think it's right?" Sergio continued. "In my day—"

"In your day," Marcella interrupted him, "people did far worse both by day and by night."

"You heard that, Annamaria? Do you think that's the way for a girl to talk to her dad?" Sergio said to his wife, who was reduced now to a crumple of rags kept together by sparse curlers. "Eh? Is that any way to treat your father?" The tone of Sergio's voice was taking an acrid turn, tempers were starting to flare, and the stage seemed set for a late-night *sceneggiata napoletana* – a performance of shrieking and passion in which Francesco had had plenty of opportunity to take part in the past.

But the telephone started to ring. Their gazes fell on that grey object that had never made so bold, in the course of its long existence, as to go off after half-past ten at night – except once, six years before, when it had announced the passing to a better life of granddad Michele. No one dared to pick up the receiver, and they all stood there rooted to the floor.

In the end, after at least a dozen rings, Marcella stepped over to it and answered.

"Hello?"

There followed a long silence. Sergio was staring slack-jawed at his daughter. Annamaria had huddled back into the gloom of the bedroom and looked on with terror-dazed eyes, expecting some dreadful news. Francesco remained at the far end of the corridor, his right arm leaning against the wall and his legs crossed.

"*Sì… sì… sì…*" Marcella kept saying at regular intervals. She then added: "Yes, he's here… I'll pass him over to you…"

She looked up and stared at her brother. "It's for you."

All eyes were now on Francesco. He wobbled towards the telephone, as a hundred thoughts whirled through his mind – fragments of conversations, faces, images – like when one is half-awake. Who could be calling him at such a late hour?

"Yes?" he said, taking the receiver.

"Franziskus!" shouted a voice at the other end, and Francesco had the impression he could see a piratical profile twisted into a familiar grimace. For a few moments he was struck dumb, as his parents and sister continued to gaze at him in amazement.

"I bet you were asleep," continued the voice. "Wakey wakey! Up and at 'em! What's wrong with you? Always sleeping. It's not even midnight – the night's young, man."

"It's nearly one," Francesco whispered.

There was a moment's silence.

"Ah, must've forgotten to put my watch forward – ha ha."

"How did you get this number?"

"I looked up your surname in the local phone book. There was only one number, which wasn't the one you gave me, so… bingo."

"I wasn't expecting your call."

"Sorry, mate. I need a small favour."

Francesco remained silent.

"Do you think I could leave a few boxes at your place for a few days? I'll pop by and pick them up later. Just a few books, you know, nothing heavy…"

"Sure, no problem," Francesco said.

"Thanks, pal. And… listen, is there any chance you could put me up for two or three days? Just to give me time to sort out a few things in Rome, then I'll be off…"

"Well, sure, but look – couldn't we talk about it tomorrow? No offence, but… it's late and—"

"Oh, I see…" said Pierre.

Francesco sighed. "Where are you now?"

"I'm in a phone box in the main piazza of Genzano. There's a coffee bar on my left, a phallic fountain in front of me and—"

"I know where you are. Wait there, I'll be over in ten-fifteen minutes."

As Francesco hung up, his father started to shout.

"Who the hell's that then? Do you think this is any time to phone people's homes?"

"Sergio, calm down. They'll start knocking on the ceiling."

"I don't give a damn about those old goats downstairs. A man can't even fart in his own home these days. You've seen your children? I have no authority in this house any more. No authority at all. And you, Goldilocks" – he pointed at Marcella – "I can't wait for you to clear the bloody hell out of here, you hear me? And you too, you scrounging little shirker. Sod off."

"Don't make so much noise, Sergio," his wife pleaded. "Rosa'll start whacking her broomstick on the wall."

"She won't."

"Oh yes she will. She's not deaf, you know."

"I don't care."

Marcella edged past her father and, with a defiant wink, slipped into the bathroom to remove her make-up. It was Francesco's turn to call down the paternal wrath on his head that night, and it was twenty minutes before he could escape to collect Pierre.

12

Genzano

FRANCESCO TOOK PIERRE to his flat in the old medieval town, which had belonged to his late grandparents Lina and Michele, and which he was now using by arrangement with his mum and Aunt Teresa – on strict condition that no strangers should be allowed in. As they walked up the steep street of the Infiorata, Pierre told him that on returning to the San Lorenzo flat he'd found all his things packed up in boxes down in the porter's lodge, and the locks on the door changed.

"You've been evicted?" Francesco asked.

"Come on, be serious. No one gets evicted in Italy."

"What then?"

"I don't know. I need to find out. But I have a hunch who did it. The porter says he knows nothing – *nulla vidi*. He's from Sicily."

"Why didn't you call the *carabinieri*? It's your flat. Can anyone just kick you out like that?"

"Well," Pierre said, "it's complicated. The flat's not in my name. I don't pay the rent. I only use it from time to time when I'm in Rome. It belongs to an old friend of mine. Don't worry about it, I'll sort it out. I'll sort everything out."

Francesco's place was filled with a strong smell of beeswax and furniture polish. His mother took turns with Aunt Teresa to clean it, and he had a feeling that there was a secret battle of wills waged between them, and that they were trying to outdo each other in keeping it as immaculate and fresh-smelling as possible. As a result, after the death of Nonna Lina three years before, the flat had been turned into a kind of Buddhist temple and, although he now lived there, Francesco was afraid of moving a single chair out of place. He offered Pierre his sofa bed in the dining room, under a cheap print of the Mona Lisa, and settled down on the king-sized bed in what used to be his grandparents' bedroom.

The heat, the hard mattress, the late hour, as well as a coda of thoughts and emotions following the scene at his parents', were getting in the way of sleep, and Francesco kept twisting and turning under the sheets. It must have been close to two thirty when all of a sudden he thought he could smell a whiff of smoke. He sprang out of bed and tiptoed into the corridor. The smell was stronger there, and he could see a faint light under the dining-room door. He opened it with caution and saw Pierre sitting by the closed window in the dark, cigarette in hand, a greyish cloud around him, outlined by the orange glow of a neon lamp-post.

"Pierre," he whispered.

"Who are you?" There was a silence. "Who am I, for that matter?"

"What are you doing?"

"Chewing the cud of sweet and bitter fancy."

"If my mum or my aunt comes here tomorrow, I'll be mince-meat – potato peelings."

"What, just for a bit of ash on the floor?"

"Marsyas was flayed alive for much much less."

"Shall I put out the cigarette?"

"That would be a good start. And open the window, please."

Francesco switched on the light and saw an empty bottle of Vecchia Romagna and a half-empty one of Cointreau on the table. Something within him shuddered.

"Do you want to… imbibe?" Pierre asked in a casual tone.

"You've… you've not…"

"It's lost a bit of its flavour, but it's still drinkable."

"Then you really want me dead."

"Don't worry, I'll buy you two new bottles tomorrow."

"Are you drunk?"

"Me? Drunk? Nah. Just needed a nightcap."

"I wonder how you can always stay up at night."

"I wonder how you can *sleep* at night." Pierre stubbed the cigarette out in the crystal ashtray on the table and opened the window. "Not just you, everyone. The whole world."

Making sure the operation was soundless, Francesco pulled out a chair from under the table and sat across from Pierre.

"Is anything the matter?"

"Whoa, you're staring at me as if I'm on suicide watch."

"Well, it's just that you look a bit frazzled – are you all right?"

"Yes, it's all just lovely here." He lit up another cigarette.

"Are you worried about something?"

"Nah. My gran used to be a worrier. She'd wake up in the middle of the night to pick up figs and cherries because she was afraid that birds would get there first in the morning. Me, I'm easy: I never worry about anything."

"OK, so we can all peacefully go to bed now."

"She's a testy bitch."

"What? Who?"

"Vanessa. She's an angry person. Seriously. I've got a picture of her here. Look. Look at her face – her tight jowls, her body language. She brims with negativity. And she's a frosty fuck, like all Germans."

"OK, you're drunk. Let's talk tomorrow morning, all right?"

"Do you want to know what's wrong with my life at the moment? Nothing. Nothing at all. To put it in a poetical way, it's shit-besprent. I've got too many debts."

"Debts?"

"An Everest's worth. I've gambled fortunes away. I'm in arrears with three mortgages. Four, actually. I've spread myself over too much bread. The thing is, I've got millions offshore, but can't get to my money right now. It's too late."

"Yes, it's too late, I agree. Let's go to bed."

"What bothers me is that you're sitting all comfortable under a tree out in the country, breathing in the fresh air, listening to the birds singing – and after five minutes out pops a peasant with a twelve-bore in his hand: 'Oi, you, get off my fucking land!' But if you tell him you're the nephew of the Mayor, he'll apologize and the next day will come trotting along to give you a carton of eggs."

"You're not making sense. Come on. Pillow time."

"You think I'm talking nonsense? Look, it's as easy as pie: the secret is to *use* money, not *own* money, OK?"

"No, I'm not following you. Tomorrow, maybe." Francesco got up.

"OK, OK, don't worry, you'll get your head round it sooner or later. Go to sleep, go to sleep. You should do a Masters in sleeping, by the way. I promise I won't drop ash everywhere. And I'll clear the table. Tell me, where do you keep the fire extinguishers? Ha ha. See you tomorrow." Something red and glowing slipped from Pierre's fingers and disappeared into the folds of night.

"Goodnight," Francesco whispered, and started to close the door, but then he opened it again. "Are you sure you're all right?"

"I'm good. Boy, am I good. Did you hear on the telly? That convict, the one who murdered his wife and children with a hammer and then buried them in a compost-filled bath, he bought a lottery ticket and won ten-and-a-half billion lire the other day. Do you think it's fair?"

"Goodnight," Francesco replied, closing the door behind him. He sneaked back to his grandparents' bedroom and fell asleep in a matter of minutes.

The next morning, when Francesco awoke, Pierre was back to his spruce-and-shaven cheerful self, with sunglasses perched over his forehead.

"You don't just have mosquitoes here – you've got real fighter jets. Just look what they've done to me." And he showed Francesco his forearm, dotted with a cluster of red swellings. "The Roman ones don't bite – the smog knocks them off first."

"They gave me no bother at all," Francesco said, looking at his unbitten arms.

"It's because *I* have the finest-quality blood – *c'ho 'r sangue bbono, io*," Pierre said. "That's why all the mosquitoes and vampires and Vanessas rush to me."

They had breakfast down at the Caffè Nazionale, walked down the Corso, then uphill to the Olmata boulevard and back to the medieval *borgo* of Genzano Vecchio huddled around the Palazzo Sforza-Cesarini and overlooking Lake Nemi. They brought in all the boxes from Pierre's car under the watchful eye of Francesco's neighbours, who pretended to be engaged in early-morning window-to-window conversation, hung clothes on the lines or watered plants on their small balconies.

"I've got some more stuff to pick up in Rome," said Pierre, once the last carton had been carried inside. "Not much, just a couple of truckloads. Only joking. You coming along?"

"I think I'll stay here to sort out these boxes, if it's all right."

"OK. I shouldn't be too long. I'll be back around noon. I'll let you buy me lunch and show me the local amenities."

"Why not."

As Pierre sped off in his car, Francesco went back into the flat to tidy it up and give the rooms a good airing. He noticed that some of the boxes contained multiple copies of books written by an author called Lele Fante – i.e. the "Elephant" – in all probability Pierre's nom de plume.

He pulled out a few volumes and started to leaf through them with curiosity. The first was an essay entitled *On Tonsures*, which purported to be the translation of an anonymous medieval manuscript, *De tonsurarum natura*, that had only just been discovered in an old Benedictine monastery. The book's main argument was that it was possible to deduce a monk's personality from the shape and size of his shaved crown. The introduction, notes and engravings drew attention to the revolutionary scope of this treatise, which did not just pre-date by several centuries Giambattista della Porta's *De humana physiognomonia*, but anticipated Lavater's studies on pathognomy, Gall's phrenology and Lombroso's system of criminal physiognomy, and opened up a whole new field of science examining and interpreting men's bald patches.

The second book, called *Italian Graffiti*, consisted of a comparative analysis of the inscriptions discovered on the walls of Pompeii and Herculaneum and the ones to be found in the railway underpasses of modern cities – "*Oppi, emboliari, fur, furuncule*", "Gavazzini, thief and clown!"; "*Myrtis bene felas*", "Giovannona's a filthy cow", etc. – showing how certain manifestations of human sensibility were universal and more authentic and heartfelt than the lines of many of the great poets we study and revere.

There was a novel entitled *The Day of the Jackass*, another one called *How to Do Kama-Sutra in a Gas Mask*, and a collection of stories, plays and even poetry, in which stood out lines such as:

I came to birth *sub Silvio* Berlusconi,
in the land of corruption and baloney.

In these volumes, Francesco could hear and see, almost in every word, the unique voice and unmistakeable Levantine face of Pierre – his humour, sometimes coarse, sometimes silly and sometimes acerbic, and his whimsical elaborations leading to the inevitable punchline.

The phone rang, and Francesco hurried down the corridor in the hope it would be Chloe.

"Hello?"

"Hi Francesco. So you're back?"

"You're very good at the obvious, Leo."

"You had a good time? How was your diaspora?"

That was Leonardo's peculiar way of talking: he loved to replace one word by another that often had very little to do with it. Francesco did the same when speaking to him.

"My diaspora was all right, thanks. Shame you turkeyed out and didn't come along. We could've had some fun together. I hope you've asked your mum's imprimatur before calling me."

"Very amusing."

"So how's your latest novel going?"

"Just finished writing it. It's good. Much better than my previous three attempts. I'll give it to you to read. But I'm curious to hear about your exodus."

Francesco told him about the various stages in his travels and some of the people he'd met, from his adventures in Germany to his vicissitudes in Sweden, Denmark, Holland, England and France, right up to his feats at the Monte Carlo casino and his journey back at the wheel of a Maserati Biturbo.

"Whoa. How much did you win, then?" Leonardo asked.

"It wasn't my car. It belongs to this guy I met in Munich."

"Is he rich? What does he do?"

"Oh, he's… he's a… he's a writer, just like yourself, in fact. Does the name Lele Fante mean anything to you?"

There was a short silence.

"Are you taking the Mickey Mouse? Would that be *the* Lele Fante? The author of *Watermelons Are on a Roll*?"

"Why, is he famous?"

"What do you mean 'famous'? He's my totem!"

"Your totem? Oh, I see – your idol."

"Is he there with you now? Can you introduce me to him? Perhaps he could read my novel and give me an endorsement."

"Calm down, calm down." Francesco smiled as he pictured his friend's face. Leonardo was the epitome of every aspiring writer, and had all the necessary requirements to become, some day, a *real* one: an intellectual's glasses, an artist's earring and the long, tousled locks of a poet. With qualities such as these, combined with a dose of resilience and stubbornness, he was sure to go very far, especially in a country like Italy, where there is such a dearth of writers and poets. "He's not here," Francesco continued, "but he's doing a book launch tomorrow at the Libreria del Corso, so if you want to meet him perhaps you could come along."

"What time?"

"Around six, I think."

"I'll be there at five. I'll also bring my book of *poemata*."

"Don't. I think your magnum opus will be more than enough."

"All right, all right. You're so funny, Francesco. You stand there, cool as a turnip, and tell me you've driven four hundred miles in Lele Fante's car, just like that – as if it's nothing special? Did you really not know who he was?"

Francesco was about to answer: "I still don't know who he really is," but then ended the conversation by saying goodbye and arranging to meet his friend the following day at the bookshop in Rome.

He went back to his grandparents' bedroom and opened the white cupboard that occupied the full length of the far wall, to see if he could hide the boxes in there. As he was moving stuff around in the stale, naphthalene-rich interior of the cupboard, he came across an old shoebox brimful of photos and papers. He emptied its contents on the bed and started to analyse them.

Some of the photos he recognized: he remembered seeing them when he was younger. But others were new to him. There was a faded Polaroid of him with his sister at the seaside aged three or four, a picture of him playing the recorder during a school show, another one where he was dressed up as Harlequin. There was also a bunch of black-and-white photos of his mum and dad going back to when they were not married. In those quadrangles of frozen time, they looked young and happy, they seemed to look forward to the days ahead of them, to the bright prospect of their future together. The papers were letters his parents had exchanged during Sergio's short stay in the barracks of Barletta. They were full of tenderness, care and affection. One letter from his dad read: "I cant wate to cum back home. I luv you more than werds can say." They were a loving couple. They were beautiful. What had happened to them? Why and when had their lives taken a wrong turn?

From the box had also emerged a few random objects, such as a small chess set, a large glass marble, an old coin and a pack of tarot cards, with which he had played so many times as a boy. Francesco picked up the marble and looked through its variegated core in search of a shape he could recognize, but was unable to see one. He then took the coin and observed it near the window. It was a small one-lira piece dating from the year he was born, from a series which had now petered out. He flipped it onto the bed, and it came out on the cornucopia side rather than the one showing the scales. That might mean that a life of abundance – not one of balanced predictability – was lying in store for him. After such an auspicious result, it was with reluctant hands that Francesco slid the tarots out of their case.

The first card he turned was the Juggler, symbol of skilfulness and deceit. The second major arcanum to come out, after a few minor ones, was the Wheel. Next appeared, in quick succession, the Papess and the Empress, which by an uncanny coincidence were followed by a third woman, the Queen of Pentacles. Francesco stopped and reflected. In what direction was Fortune's wayward hand pointing? What would be the next arcanum to be revealed? Would it be Justice or the Judgement, as he feared, or – worse still – the Devil or the most dreaded tarot, Number Thirteen, the emblem of Death? Francesco kept turning cards with apprehension – the Five of Wands, the Three of Cups, the Nine of Swords – and a smile of relief appeared on his face as the Lovers finally came out, facing upright.

It was only then that he realized that someone was honking the horn outside. He went to the window and signalled to Pierre that he'd be down in a minute.

13

The Alban Hills, Tivoli

WHEN FRANCESCO GOT OUT, he found Pierre pacing up and down the street, smoking a cigarette, looking nervous.

"Shall we get the boxes in?" Francesco asked.

"No, we'll do it later. Let's go."

"Where?"

"Somewhere, it doesn't matter. Let's get out of here. I think I'm being tailed."

"You're what?"

"Two guys in a silver Alfetta. They look dodgy."

"You sure?"

"Positive. And I don't like it. Jump in."

They drove away down the cobblestones of the old town, until they joined the Appian Way and headed south, towards Velletri. At the junction for Nemi, Pierre made an abrupt turn left.

"Steady, man!" Francesco shouted, as the car hit a small pothole. "You see those cypresses on the left? That's the local cemetery. I'd rather not visit it just yet."

"I only want to test their mettle."

Pierre switched to fourth gear and pushed the gas pedal down hard.

"Man, please, please!" pleaded Francesco, holding on to his seat. "Do you know how many people die on this road each year?"

But Pierre didn't reply, driving as fast as hell, entering even the most dangerous bends up the slopes of Lake Nemi at anything between eighty and ninety kilometres an hour, with Francesco crying "We're gonna roll over!", "We're gonna jack-knife!" and "Aaaaaaah!"

They continued at racing speeds past Nemi and down the Via dei Laghi, and Pierre began to slow down only when they were climbing up the steep road to Marino.

"I think I've lost them," Pierre said with a satisfied smirk.

"I think I'm feeling sick."

They stopped in Frascati and parked the car in an inconspicuous spot near the train station. After eating at a *fraschetta*, where a group of drunken Germans were improvising folk songs to the puzzled amusement of the locals, they strolled through the town centre for a while and enjoyed a visit to the magnificent Villa Aldobrandini, although Pierre kept casting vigilant looks around him all the time. Late in the afternoon they headed back to the car.

"Shall we return to Genzano?" asked Francesco.

"I'd rather wait until it's dark."

"Where shall we go then?"

"Tivoli. It's been years since I've been."

This time Pierre drove slowly and, also because of the traffic, they got there a whole hour later. Back to his old ways, Pierre double-parked the car right in the historic centre of town.

"Won't it get towed away?" Francesco tried.

"We're not in London any more," Pierre replied. "And they don't see a Maserati every day around these parts: they'll be too scared to touch it."

They drank a coffee in a nearby café and went for a long walk through old Tivoli, first passing the church of Santa Maria Maggiore and then the Annunziata. From there they descended a long flight of steps to Piazza Campitelli, the ancient Campus Metelli. Then they turned back and made their way down streets and alleys until they reached the Temple of Vesta on the Tiburtine acropolis, which overhangs a vast valley, and from where it is possible to see the picturesque waterfalls of the Aniene river.

Their next stop was the Villa d'Este. After a quick tour of the grandiose palace decorated with overblown mannerist frescoes, they wandered through the paths of the "Garden of Wonders", admiring the fountains, the grottoes, the watercourses, the hydraulic music and all the other virtuoso examples of sculpture and architecture that sprang from the genius of Pirro Ligorio. Pierre's mood had improved, but then, just as he finished telling Francesco a dirty joke about Pinocchio rubbing one out with sandpaper, he froze in his steps, and his expression darkened.

"What the hell?" he whispered.

"What?" Francesco said.

"There's a guy following us," Pierre said, lifting his sunglasses.

"Where?"

"He's slipped off now. He was standing over there" – he gave a jerk with his head – "by that fountain – a bloke with a white shirt and a hat. I saw him tagging along after us inside the villa."

"I think you're being paranoid now."

"I'm not. I'm dead certain. Don't look round: act natural, act natural. Keep your eyes skinned."

They headed back down the garden paths, walking with a stiff gait, and after a while Pierre whispered to Francesco through a corner of his mouth:

"There he is, see him?... Don't turn round, don't turn round... see him?"

"How can I see him if I don't turn round?" But he had caught sight of him now, the man with the white shirt and the hat.

"Pretend you haven't seen him," Pierre kept whispering, as they headed to the exit. "Walk fast."

They rushed back to the car and sped away through the outskirts of town.

"Where are we going?" Francesco asked.

"I want to see if they are still behind us."

Once they were doing a hundred down the Via Tiburtina and calm seemed to have been restored, Pierre exclaimed:

"There it is, the silver Alfetta. Shit. Must be professionals."

"But who are they?"

"Who knows? Private eyes? Hitmen? The FBI? You tell me. An angry woman is capable of anything. Now hold tight!"

The speedometer jumped to the 130 mark, and after a near-collision, a lunge through a red light and two do-or-die blind overtakings, Pierre braked and swerved into a narrow country road. A few minutes later, as Francesco was recovering his ability to breathe and feel his body, he realized that they had reached Hadrian's Villa. They parked behind a huge

German coach so as not leave the car visible, then hurried to the entrance.

"They won't catch us here," Pierre said with a wink. "This is a big old place."

The elderly woman at the ticket booth pointed out that it was only half an hour until closing time.

"No problem, miss," said Pierre, treating her to a wink too, "we'll let you go home on time."

The evening shadows were beginning to extend across the Campagna Romana. The crickets chirruped again in the dry grass, and a thin sliver of moon – little more than a watery reflection until a few minutes earlier – was shining a feeble light against the expanse of the sky wrapped in the pinkish haze from the setting sun.

They hurried up the avenue of cypresses that led to the massive wall of the Poikile. In the expanse beyond, a few sunburnt tourists could still be seen wandering around or casting curious glances at the greenish waters of the pond. As they made their way through dilapidated Roman brick-work, uneven marble floors and column stumps, Pierre and Francesco often looked round to see if the man with the white shirt and the hat was following them.

The ruins had taken on an eerie look, as if filled with the shadows of ages past. A light breeze was picking up from the west, and from time to time a rustle from the trees swept through the deepening twilight.

"It's getting late," Francesco said, observing that the place had become deserted.

"Don't worry," Pierre said, as he lit up a cigarette, "no one's gonna mind if we stay a little longer."

They walked past a series of brown edifices that seemed to be standing only thanks to modern scaffolding, and found themselves in an open space with tall buildings all around. The evening was continuing to darken, making it difficult to distinguish the outlines of things.

"Everyone's left already, let's go back," Francesco said, with a trace of unease in his voice. "There's hardly any moonlight. It gets dark quickly in the countryside."

"Five minutes," Pierre said, stretching his open palm. "Five minutes and we'll be off. You're not scared, are you?"

"Me? Scared? I'm not—" Francesco turned round, and could no longer see his friend. "Pierre!" he whispered. "Pierre! Where are you?"

"Pssst. Pssst!" a shadow called, crouched behind a wall. "Come here, come here," Pierre hissed, waving Francesco over. "I've seen him," he said, squeezing Francesco's arm.

"Seen who?"

"The guy with the hat. The hitman. There, behind us."

"Where?"

"There, inside that ruin."

"You might be wrong."

"No, no. I've seen him. I'm telling you."

"What do we do now?"

"Get out of this place."

"How? Where?" It was so dusky that Francesco could hardly see his friend's face.

"Follow me," Pierre hissed, and started padding forward with caution ahead of him.

They went up some stairs, which at some point were obstructed by the long branches of a tree. When they reached the top, they could command a vast, dark view of Villa Adriana.

"Where are we?" Francesco murmured.

"I don't know."

"We'll fall off if we're not careful."

"We won't. There he is." He was pointing at a vague spot of whiteness moving around the glittery surface of the Canopus. "Let's go back down."

They descended the steps and found themselves in a pitch-dark underground passage that stank of moss and damp. Over their heads, every so often, rectangles of starry sky opened up. In the darkest spots Pierre found his way with the help of his cigarette lighter, cursing whenever he bumped into something or stumbled on the irregular ground. Then they emerged into the open and slipped – shadows in the night – from one building to the next before diving down into another passageway, this time without any openings and much longer than the first one.

"You sure we're going the right way?" Francesco whispered.

The flicker of the lighter illuminated Pierre's face, and his cheek seemed to be affected by a slight tremor as he winked at him.

"Have faith," he said, and the light went out.

They continued to make their way down the passage, but at the end of the tunnel they found they were up against a solid wall dripping with moisture, with no way out. Pierre lifted his lighter up and waved it round a good few times, but it was no use: it was a dead end. They were trapped. They'd have to go back.

"What's that noise?" hissed Pierre, his voice cracking.

"What? Where?" Francesco said, afraid that someone could jump on them in the darkness at any moment.

"And what's this smell?" Pierre said after a few more steps, flickering the lighter around. "You shat yourself?" The light went out again and the vaults of the passage echoed to Pierre's chuckles.

Three minutes later they emerged out of the tunnel. They went up the stairs again and joined a fenced path overlooking the ruins. But they had not gone a few paces when Pierre froze.

"Who's that?"

"Where?"

"Down there. Ahead of us."

"Must be Banquo's ghost. You're imagining things."

"*Scappa! Scappa!*"

They scarpered back down the path, Pierre leading the way in the near-complete darkness, until he turned left and stepped over a low chain-link fence that had been knocked down by a tree or by vandals.

"Careful," Pierre hissed, "there could be some barbed wire."

"Use the lighter."

"Shh. They'll see us."

A fierce barking noise erupted in the distance.

"Dogs!" was Francesco's muffled shout.

"Just follow me in silence. Grr… woof!"

"Very funny."

They crossed long stretches of rough grassland, moist with the evening dew, climbed over hedges and fences, and finally managed to return to the empty car park where, a bit further down from Pierre's Maserati, under a lamp-post, stood a silver Alfetta.

"Wait here a sec," Pierre said as soon as they reached his car. He opened the boot and pulled a screwdriver out of the toolbox.

"What are you going to do?" Francesco asked, but Pierre had already disappeared without giving him an answer.

He was back in a matter of moments, and they were soon speeding off again towards the main street. Pierre kept glancing at the rear mirror and, with the voice of a drill sergeant taunting his new recruits, shouted, "OK, heroes, so you wanted to catch the enemy? Great job – pity you got caught, big shots. The Taurus is in Uranus – and does it hurt! *Mute le schegge, mute!*"

He burst into a fit of lung-splitting laughter.

14

Genzano, Rome

THE EVENTS OF THAT EVENING had no time to cohere in Francesco's mind. The next morning, when his mother phoned at ten to eight, he got one of those dressing-downs that are usually reserved for very small children.

"Is that any way to behave? *Te si 'mmattitu?* Your father's right. You've just got back and you go mucking around day and night, bringing strangers home, eh?"

Someone, in all probability Giuseppina, the wheelchair-bound neighbour who seemed to be forever keeping a lookout from her tiny kitchen window, must have tipped off Aunt Teresa.

Francesco remained silent.

"Comare Pia called me. She found cigarette stubs in her yard. You've been smoking?"

"No, it's this friend of mine. Just a cigarette or two, with all the windows open."

Pierre appeared from his room and mouthed, "Are you in trouble?" Nodding, Francesco mouthed *"Cazzi amari"* in reply and waved him away.

"And who is it, this friend of yours?"

"He and his wife put me up when I was in Germany. They've been very nice. He's only staying another day or two."

The word "wife" triggered positive associations in Annamaria's mind, and she relented.

"Aren't you coming over for lunch?" she said.

"Can I bring my friend too?"

"Yes, yes, but I won't have time to do anything special."

"Doesn't matter. A plate of pasta will do."

Of course they didn't get off with just a plate of pasta, but received the full treatment. For starters the table of the dining room – which was hardly ever used by Francesco's parents, since they rarely had guests – groaned with an array of trays and dishes containing spit-roasted pig from Ariccia, San Daniele prosciutto, mortadella, dried sausages from Norcia, green olives and other appetizers. The first course was tagliatelle with forest mushrooms – mushrooms that had been picked the night before by their neighbour Gioacchino, as Francesco's mother explained – the first of the season. The second course was spare ribs, tripe and roasted quail, with a side serving of green beans and potatoes with vinegar, mixed-leaf field salad and artichokes *alla giudìa* – then the dessert, fruit, dry figs and coffee. The whole thing was accompanied by two bottles of wine.

"Not the kind you get from the supermarkets," Annamaria pointed out with a wan smile, sitting on the edge of her chair towards the end of the meal. *"Chell'è vinaccio de bastone."*

Sergio – unshaven, ruffled, still sulking about the events of two days ago – did not say a word throughout the entire lunch. He studied Pierre with a taut scowl and an air of studied detachment. He'd put on his filthiest vest – perhaps out of obstinacy or resentment, perhaps as a protest against the world and life in general – and continued to clean his fingernails at table with a toothpick. Only when the liqueurs were brought in did he break his silence.

"Try a drop of this."

"What is it?" Pierre said, holding out his glass.

"Vogda."

"Vodka?"

"Vogda."

"The real stuff?"

"From Russia with love."

Pierre had a long sip from his glass and let the vodka slosh around in his mouth as if it was mouthwash.

"Mmm," he said at length, gulping it down. "Not bad."

"Not bad?" Sergio said with a grimace.

"Yeah, it's good."

"This is not *good*," Sergio scoffed, "this is fifty-thousand-a-bottle good. Can you play *scopa* by any chance?"

"I know the rules."

So they spent the following two hours playing cards, and since the vodka was in due course supplemented by *toscani* and whisky and Sergio was often the winner, the atmosphere became friendlier and more relaxed.

"I think it's time to go," Francesco reminded his friend when the clock was turning five. "It'll take us an hour to get there."

"Plenty of time. I'm driving. Relax."

ALESSANDRO GALLENZI

When they arrived at the Libreria del Corso, the day had not cooled down yet, and only three people had turned up, including Leonardo. The minute he clapped eyes on Francesco and his hero, he started to shimmy and caracole around them at a certain distance, hoping to be introduced.

The heat inside was even more stifling and intolerable than the weather outside, since the air conditioning wasn't working – and in Rome, if anything seizes up during or in the run-up to the long summer break, you'd better cross yourself and wait until September. To make up for this, there were half a dozen fans whirring in every corner of the bookshop, giving the impression that the room might take off any minute now.

Pierre, annoyed by the sultry humidity and the sparseness of the audience, strode past the fifty or so seats arranged in straight lines in front of the podium and went up to the bookshop manager, a stocky guy with a red face and wispy brown beard, who was testing the microphone.

"*Ba, ba, prova, prova.*"

"Are you the bookshop manager?" Pierre said in a curt tone.

"*Ba, ba.*"

"Hello?"

"One second. *Ba, ba.*"

Pierre snatched the microphone from him and started to sing:

"*Ba, ba, baciami piccina sulla bo, bo, bocca piccolina…* What is this, a singing competition?"

"I'm trying out… err… the mic."

Pierre turned to Francesco with a grin.

"Great sense of humour." He turned back to the bookshop manager. "I won't need a microphone. We can fit everyone in the front row."

"Err… More people… err… will turn up. Err… it's still early… err… ten minutes to go."

"More people. How many? Six? Seven? Do you think I've come all the way from England to present my book to a handful of losers? Whose idea was this? Eh? Who had the bright idea of doing a book launch in Rome at the end of July – without air conditioning? It's criminal. The only 'launches' you can do at this time of year are the dives into the Tiber from Cavour Bridge."

"Well, err… those actually… err… happen on New Year's Day."

"Oh do they? And why couldn't we have my launch during that time, when people actually *go* to bookshops and *buy* books and are not on holiday or thinking about sea, sailing and beach umbrellas?"

"Because, err… today, err… is the publication date."

Pierre shook his head with a peculiar smile. His brow was dripping with sweat.

"The truth is that some people couldn't organize a piss-up in a brewery. Sorry, but I'm not doing a launch in these conditions."

A skinny shop assistant, who seemed to be wilting in the heat, came up to Pierre.

"Would you like a drink?"

"No, I'd like to be somewhere else."

And he swung round, only to be confronted by Leonardo, who had been hovering behind him waiting for an opportunity to talk.

"Hi there, I'm a friend of Francesco."

"Delighted," said Pierre, and strode off.

Leonardo didn't lose hope and scurried after him.

"I'm a writer too. I've written short stories, poems and a play," he continued unperturbed.

Pierre halted and looked him in the eyes.

"How wonderful. I'm so pleased. You wouldn't happen to have them with you, would you?"

"Funny you should mention that. I've just finished a novel, and I thought you might like to have a look at it and let me know what you think. No obligation, of course. I can give it to you now, if you wish. The short stories and the poems I can send you some other time. I'm a great admirer of your work."

"Wonderful. I'm so honoured. Is there a chance we can talk about it after the reading?" Shaking his head and rolling his eyes, Pierre walked outside and lit up a cigarette.

Over the next ten minutes the bookshop began to fill up, although with a somewhat miscellaneous audience, dominated by retired schoolteachers, Japanese tourists and little old ladies dressed in black, a category of people seen in great numbers in any big Italian city during the hot months of summer. No one seemed to know anyone else, and they all sat alone with one or two empty seats between them, staring ahead with wan, expressionless faces.

When the last latecomers had found a place to sit, the bookshop manager opened the presentation.

"Err... It is an honour... err..." he began, stroking down the brown wisps of his straggly beard, "we are really proud to have... err... the great writer... Lele Fante. His works have enjoyed great success... err... have been translated in many languages..."

"Twelve," pointed out Pierre.

"Twelve… and, err… we're here today… err… to present his latest book… err… *Le nozze di Sfigaro, or The Marriage of Mr Jinx…* which no doubt will become… err… a new best-seller… and you can buy it today for… err… a special price of ten thousand lire. But I'll leave it to… err… the author to… err… talk to you about his new book. Ladies and gentlemen… err… Lele Fante."

There followed a heavy silence – nothing, not even a scatter of encouraging applause, just a brief cough from an old man.

Pierre let his gaze travel around the twenty-odd pillars of salt in front of him and got to his feet.

"Well, ladies and gentlemen, given the heat and the broken air conditioning, you'll have to admit that not only does it never rain in Rome, but it never rains but it pours…"

The frigid silence with which his attempt at a joke was greeted left him at a loss and wondering how many foreigners were in the room. The old man coughed again. Pierre seized a copy of his book from the pile on the table and turned to his audience with a strained, uncomfortable grimace on his lips. Those motionless monoliths looked back at him, inert and passive. One little old lady in the third row seemed to have gone to a better place already, judging from her closed eyes and the greenish tint of her skin. For a moment, Francesco thought that his friend might walk out, but Pierre was too much of a natural-born performer to give up.

Fired by a new inspiration, he gave a confident stare at the audience and started to read: "'*Fiat lux*,' said God in the beginning, making a mental note to speak to Agnelli, the Lamb of God. And there was light. He then created the stars, the earth and the seas, the grass and the fruit, fish, fowl and animals, man and woman. At that point He stopped, scratched his white beard and said to Himself: 'Hang on. I sense trouble ahead. Can I take this last bit back?' But it was too late, so with reluctance He said: 'All right, folks, be fruitful, multiply, replenish the earth, subdue it, have dominion over the fish, the fowl and every other living thing, blah blah blah. But please, please, don't give each other Hell – there's time for that, and I still haven't invented it.' Unfortunately, God's word never fell on deafer ears."

For some reason, everyone laughed at that, including Leonardo, who did so snorting through his nostrils, as if he was blowing his nose. Pierre went on reading with a spirited gleam in his eyes, swaying left and right, gesticulating, adding emphasis to his words, pausing and changing the expression of his face. The audience became spellbound throughout the reading and laughed at every joke or innuendo by the author – until they erupted into a final, liberating burst of applause.

"Thank you, thank you," the bookshop manager said. "We can... err... open it up to questions now. Anyone... yes, the gentleman on the left."

"Are you in any way related to John Fante, the American novelist?"

Pierre thought for a moment.

"Funnily enough, no," he said. "But the writer Rino Ceronte is a near relation of mine. We used to live together in Africa a while back."

Leonardo leant over and whispered in Francesco's ear:

"Did you get it? Rino Ceronte... 'Rhinoceros'."

"Genius," was Francesco's comment.

"Any other... err... questions?" the bookshop manager continued.

A girl in the second row stood up.

"I'd like to show some drawings, done by hand... here. I don't want to disturb you, but at the end of the talk anyone who wants... We in the Sant'Egidio community did them by hand... because I... I'm not ashamed of it, I've had a few mental problems but... the drawings are all done by hand in our free time and the teaching assistant, Andrea Bonfiglio, takes us out and... We also do other work by hand... they're all for sale... to help the community... we shouldn't be discriminated against... I'm also speaking on behalf of the others in there... thank you."

"OK, OK. Sit down, please. Do we have... err... any other questions? Otherwise we can... err... yes, the boy in the fourth row."

"I just wanted to ask Lele," said Leonardo, "if he has any advice for aspiring young writers."

Just then, the bookshop's front door creaked open. Francesco glanced back and noticed two women coming in, one with long dark hair and the other with flowing red curls, followed by a grim-looking man of mountainous build. Behind them, two more people filed in: first, the man who had been following them the day before, and after him Vanessa, in a jasper-coloured dress and black hat. Francesco turned to see Pierre's reaction.

"I'm sorry," he said, laying his book on the table. "I don't think I... well... what can I say to that..." His voice had dried up and his face had flushed crimson. "Where's the water?" he stammered, wiping his brow, and when he raised the glass to his lips his hand appeared to be trembling. "What advice can I give?" he continued, regaining a semblance of composure but still casting restless glances towards the back of the room, where five pairs of eyes had not ceased to stare at him for a moment. "I suppose my only suggestion is: be wary of your Muses, and never get married to them – some of them can turn into nasty bitches in the end. Ha ha."

Leonardo nodded as if he'd just heard a deep philosophical truth.

"I think I'm going to sign some books now," Pierre announced with a nervous smile, sitting by the table and throwing an anxious look at his watch.

There was a final round of applause, and most of the audience dispersed. As the bookshop manager and his assistant began to fold the chairs and tidy away the microphone, the electric fans and the podium, a few people came up to congratulate the author and get their copy inscribed. Vanessa was engaged in urgent confabulation with the two women and the detectives at the back of the bookshop, near the door.

When Francesco's turn arrived, he leant over and whispered to his friend:

"What are you going to do?"

"I don't know," Pierre whispered back. "But it'll be all right. Please hang around, don't leave me alone."

The last person to go up to Pierre for a dedication was Leonardo.

"Is it OK if I give you my novel now?" he said, lifting a heavy plastic bag from the floor. "It would mean so much to me."

"No, don't leave it with me: I'd lose it. I tell you what – why don't you mail it to me, together with your stories and poems?"

"Oh, thank you, thank you. Where shall I send it to?"

"Let me give you my address in England." Pierre picked up a piece of paper and scribbled over it:

61 PONCE STREET
TWATFIELD
DORKSHIRE
~~GR8 1KR~~
TO5 5ER

Francesco, glancing at the address, gave a half-smile, while Leonardo didn't seem to be able to thank his idol enough, and dashed off home to print out his poems and short stories so he would be able to send them off the very next day.

The bookshop manager and his assistant had disappeared into a back room, and Vanessa and the others now saw their chance to approach Pierre. The redhead was a mask of fury, while the dark-haired woman remained at the back of the group with downcast eyes. Of the two detectives, the one who had been wearing a hat the previous day – not just to shield himself from the sun but to cover a vast and bumpy bald patch – seemed to be in command, the other merely representing brute force. Pierre waved at all of them with an expression of innocence and a meek smile.

"How are you? Linda, Gabriella! So good to see you. Don't think for a minute I was trying to avoid you. I've been meaning to get in touch with you for months. Gabriella, you'll have your money back by tomorrow – I promise. I'll send you a cheque by recorded delivery. And don't believe anything Vanessa may have told you. Let's try to avoid a scene here, OK? Let's all go somewhere nice, sit around a table, relax and sort everything out, all right? Like civil people, with no bad feelings. I am tired of all this myself. By the way, would you like a signed copy of my new book?"

"There'll be a lot more paper for you to sign soon," said the balding detective, stroking his pockmarked nose and suppressing a smirk under his moustache.

"What was that?" Pierre said – but he had understood. "Who are these clowns?" he asked Vanessa.

"They work for me," she said, staring at Pierre from beyond her sunglasses. "Why didn't you accept my offer?"

"What offer? Ah, that. I was hoping it could be negotiable."

"It isn't."

"I see. Well, then I'm happy with it."

"You are?"

"Sure, no problems, whatever. You know I'm easy. Give me the papers and I'll sign them. In fact, I can do a special signing session for ex-wives, ha ha."

"What about *me*?" Linda said, at the top of her voice.

"What about you, darling?"

"You've destroyed my peace. You've ruined my life."

"Have I? Oh, poor little girl – smack smack Pierre. I thought you'd found enough consolation in that plucked bird of prey – that legal bald eagle, your boss, the *partner* – what was his n—"

Linda landed him a violent slap in the face.

"Ha ha ha," Pierre said, trying to laugh off the blow and bringing a hand to his cheek, while the taller detective restrained Linda. "You're in the wrong queue, sweetheart: this one's for signings, not for slappings. And even Judas greeted his master with a kiss, not a—"

"Sorry to interrupt," said the skinny assistant, with the bookshop manager standing beside her and looking on in puzzlement, "but we really have to close."

"Sure, sure," said Pierre, running a hand through his hair. "We were just rehearsing a scene from an ancient Greek tragedy. Thanks for organizing the launch. It went well, eh? We must have sold at least six or seven copies."

"Five," said the bookshop manager, yawning. "Not too bad."

Pierre shook his head and walked towards the exit. Once they were all out in the street, he was the first one to talk.

"Why don't we have a drink or dinner together?"

"Where?" said Vanessa.

"What about Rosati's in Piazza del Popolo? I'll just go and get the car round the corner and meet you there in twenty minutes."

"Your car does not exist any more," said the balding detective.

"Vanished. Eliminated. Kaput," said his companion.

"Ha ha ha," Pierre said, wagging his finger and smiling. "You haven't touched my car, have you?"

"Who started it?"

"Who started what?"

"Who slit the tyres of our car?"

"In the middle of nowhere and at that time of night," added the taller detective.

"Come on," Pierre said, laughing. "You've got a stupid Alfetta, a scrap dealer's gift. My car's actually worth something. Seriously, you haven't done anything to it, have you?"

"Well, you should have left our stupid Alfetta alone. You'll have to pay for that too. Come with us."

"Take your hands off me."

"I said come with us, this way."

"You keep your fingers in your pockets. I can walk on my own."

"*Basta*." The tall detective intervened and grabbed Pierre by the shirt collar, dragging him towards the edge of the street. "Taxi!"

They climbed into two yellow cabs – Pierre and Francesco with the two detectives and Vanessa with Linda and Gabriella. On the way, Pierre kept taunting the detectives: "I know a very good garage near Tivoli, specializes in vintage cars. I can give you their phone number. You've got a funny accent. Where do you guys come from? Let me guess: some small place in the mountains? Ciociaria? Marsica? They do very good goat's cheese up there. Is it true that people there shag sheep as a hobby?" Then he turned to Francesco. "What's that long visage, sir?"

"I'm thinking," Francesco replied.

"What are you thinking?"

"That the cards were wrong."

"Mm? What cards? Everything's going to be fine, trust me." Then he lowered his voice to a whisper: "I still have a few aces up my sleeve."

At that time of evening there wasn't much traffic about, so they managed to cover the distance to Piazza del Popolo in less than ten minutes. The two taxis drew up outside Rosati at about the same time. While the balding detective was paying the fare for one cab and the taller one for the other, Pierre whispered to Francesco:

"Lend me fifty thousand. Quick."

Francesco took out a fifty-thousand-lire note from his pocket and crumpled it into Pierre's open palm, hidden behind his back.

"Cheers. *A buon rendere*," Pierre said sotto voce.

They walked towards the entrance of Rosati: the women in front, the men behind. The first taxi had already left, and the other was about to move away when Pierre turned and shouted, "Shit. I left my book in the car…" and ran towards it, opening the door and tumbling inside as it was heading off. There was a quick crunch of tyres on the cobblestones, a rapid swerve, and off it went, vanishing from view before anyone could even realize what had happened.

Taken by surprise, the detectives exchanged incredulous looks, then a horrendous volley of oaths broke out. The women gabbled away in agitation among the curious glances of the café's customers and passers-by, while Francesco looked at the empty street and the cloud of smoke left by the taxi and smiled. That devil Pierre, that lover of *coups de théâtre*, that quick-change artist, had managed to get away yet again.

15

Rome, Genzano

WHEN THE NEXT MORNING he went to pick up Chloe at Termini, Francesco was expecting to see the girl he had met in London, and was astonished when a beautiful woman with a stream of blond hair tumbling over her shoulders, with sophisticated make-up and shiny pearl earrings, walked towards him and embraced him.

"Hi Chloe. You're... you've—"

She gave him a kiss on the lips and took him by the hand.

"*Ciao, bello*," she said.

"I like your Italian."

They dropped her bags at a hotel near the Tower of the Militia, then began a long tour on foot, starting from Trajan's Column and the Imperial Fora to the Arch of Constantine and that big piece of marble Emmental, the Coliseum, then back to Piazza Venezia, the Capitoline Museums and the Theatre of Marcellus. In the afternoon, after a long break at a café outside the Pantheon, they continued their wanderings under the glare of a merciless sun, stopping only to take a drink of cool water from a fountain or exchange a quick kiss. They strolled round Piazza Navona and Campo de' Fiori, visited Fontana di Trevi and Piazza di Spagna until, exhausted, they ended up on the Pincio Gardens, where they could sit and enjoy the fresh evening breeze while taking in one of the best views of the city.

"There's so much we haven't seen yet," Francesco said.

"Yes, but perhaps it's enough for one day."

They went back to the hotel in Via della Cordonata, and Chloe asked Francesco if he could help her bring the luggage to her room.

"I see you've got a double bedroom," Francesco said when he opened the door. "Lovely."

"Yeah, I made a mistake when I booked… Perhaps you could stay? It seems such a waste."

"I'm not used to sleeping in the same bed with someone else. I could be a nuisance."

"Who told you we'd be sleeping?"

The following day they woke up very late, had breakfast in a nearby bar and resumed their tour of the city, making St Peter's their first destination, and covering most of the remaining monuments and museums over the next few hours. In the evening, after checking out from the hotel and depositing one of Chloe's suitcases at Stazione Termini, they took the Metro to Anagnina, and from there the coach to Genzano.

The town was quiet and sleepy, except for a group of youths in the main square. As they walked up the steep Via Garibaldi and turned right towards the *borgo vecchio*, they felt the coolness of the night wrap around them and a gentle wind rustling among the trees. When they got to the square in front of Palazzo Sforza-Cesarini, they were rewarded with a magnificent moonlit scene.

"This is amazing," Chloe exclaimed, admiring the imposing façade of the building. "When was it built?"

"Oh, I'm not sure. Seventeenth, eighteenth century perhaps? But the foundations are much older: there was a medieval castle before."

"Why is it all dark inside? Is it uninhabited?"

"Yeah, it's been empty for some time. It's derelict now." Francesco scratched his nose. "My mum and her family used to live in it."

"Oh yeah? Where did you leave your horse and armour then?"

"They just *lived* here: they didn't own the place. After the war it became a shelter for people who had been evacuated or had lost their homes during the bombings."

"Posh accommodation."

"Not really. There were dozens of families living on each floor, with cardboard partitions between them and no bathrooms. This went on for over twenty years, until each family was given a council flat. Fancy a quick peek inside?"

"God, no: it's pitch-dark. I'd be afraid."

"Come on, it's safe. I played in there so many times when I was a kid."

"All right, but just for one minute, and only if you hold my hand."

Wedging themselves between two rusty door panels held together by loose chains, they emerged into the entrance hall. In front of them, suffused by the moonlight that filtered through the glassless windows of the front façade, opened the main staircase.

"Let's go up."

"What? No." Chloe shook her head, her hair glistening in the half-light.

"Please. I want to show you something."

"I'm scared."

"I swear there are no rats, ghosts or vampires."

"Yes, but the floor might crumble beneath us."

"Don't be silly. You won't be disappointed, I promise."

They went up the stairs to the first floor – Chloe following behind with cautious steps, giving out little cries whenever she bumped into a piece of rubble – then walked down a dark corridor, until they reached a large frescoed room. Its balconied windows provided a spectacular vista of Lake Nemi and its steep slopes bathed in moonlight.

"It's… it's one of the most beautiful things I've ever seen," said Chloe.

"I told you."

"What are these frescoes? I can't see them very well."

"I think it's a hunting scene. That's the lake below, and that's Diana chasing a deer."

"She looks quite stern, doesn't she?"

"She's not really interested in love or human affairs – just hunting. The lake is sacred to her: it's called the 'Mirror of Diana'."

"Why 'mirror'?"

"Why? Because Diana is also the Moon, and her face is reflected in the surface of the lake, like now. Look how glorious and serene she is."

"There's so much history around here."

"I know. So many myths, most of them forgotten."

"So how can you not like Italy?"

"Oh, I do like it. There's not an inch of my country I don't like. What infuriates me is the level of degradation it's descended to – the stupidity, the asininity of the Italian people."

"Asininity – that's a nice expression."

"You see this villa we're in? It was beautiful and full of life once – now it's a dark, dead ruin. I think it's a perfect metaphor for our nation."

"But it can be restored."

"How? By whom? No one cares, and it's too much work. One generation alone cannot repair the damage done by many."

"I don't agree. I think that the work and the ideas of even one person can make the difference."

"Yeah, right. The 'Man of Destiny'. Let's talk again in twenty years' time and see if anything has changed – or if it's got worse. Mm... there's a big cloud moving across the face of the moon. Let's go out before it becomes too dark. It's getting a bit chilly, too."

They made their way down the stairs and stopped in the main hall.

"Is it just me or can you smell a cigarette?" said Chloe.

"Perhaps it's coming from outside."

"Look, there's a smouldering butt here. Do you think some-one's been following us?"

"I doubt it, but I'd rather not hang around for too long."

They slunk out of Palazzo Sforza-Cesarini and walked under an arch into the old town. They reached Francesco's flat, and

ALESSANDRO GALLENZI

when he was about to open the door he said in an aphonic voice: "OK, now I want you to become weightless, invisible and mute. Abracadabra."

"Why?" Chloe murmured.

"You see that old-brick construction? Behind it lives a half-paralysed witch who keeps watch on this door all day – forever on the lookout."

"Really? Hello! I'm here! Nice to meet you!" shouted Chloe, waving at a small window.

"Thank you, Chloe."

He unlocked the door, switched on the corridor light and tiptoed in.

"Do you want to sing a serenade too?" he asked.

"Maybe tomorrow."

"OK, then I'll prepare the guitar and the accordion."

They undressed and lay naked on the bed, looking at how the moon progressed through the sky.

"Why don't we make our lives into a long, uninterrupted journey?" Francesco said.

"Where do you want to go?"

"Mmm… Athens, to start with."

"What about Budapest?"

"Madrid?"

"Tokyo?"

"You can't get there on InterRail."

They giggled in the dark. Francesco recounted some age-old stories and fairy tales, until they both fell asleep and the warmth of their bodies wrapped them in a cocoon of softness. When Francesco woke in the middle of the night, he only had to draw a light blanket over them, and they slept the best sleep of their

218

lives until the sun rose and the bells of Santa Maria della Cima chimed their good morrow.

It was only a few minutes past eight when Francesco descended the large steps of Via Livia to buy breakfast from one of the bars on the Corso. It was a fine morning, and the heat of noon could already be sensed gathering in the air. Francesco was a few yards from the two fountains at the bottom of the steps when he heard a loud whistle.

He stopped and looked round. Then another whistle carried through the air behind him. He peered in the direction of the Trattoria dei Cacciatori, and now, yes – sitting astride a red bicycle, sunglasses on his forehead and index fingers still wedged into the corners of his mouth – he could see Pierre staring at him with a roguish expression, in which could be read the greatest satisfaction at having caught him by surprise.

"*Stallionus Italianus*! Been horsing around, eh? Making the mares whinny? How does she like your *andouillette de Gennesanno*, your Genzanese salami?"

"Pierre," Francesco said, walking up to him and shaking his head.

"Have you had time to rest your sore groin? Look at those rings under your eyes! Come on, come on, don't tell me it's all platonic: how're you getting on with the English filly, eh? Did you get a spot of rumpy-pumpy this morning?" He made a pumping gesture with his fist, accompanying it with a sibilant whistle.

"Pierre. Pierre. What are you doing here at this hour of the morning – on that bike?"

"Do you like my new Maserati Biruota?" He lit up a cigarette and gave a big puff of smoke. "My new means of transport. I got it 'on loan'. Temporary measures."

"What's happened? They really took away your car?"

"Ah, short-term gain. They'll live to regret it. Shall we have a coffee?"

"Sure."

"*Vamos.*"

They settled down in a quiet corner of one of the cafés in the main square of the town and ordered cappuccinos, mineral water and croissants.

"Just like that morning in Munich," Pierre said, with a smile.

"Yeah. We've clocked up a few miles since then."

"And we've had some fun. Do you want a cigarette?"

"Why not?"

Without exchanging a word, they smoked and had their cappuccinos and *cornetti*. Pierre was the first to break the silence.

"So, what happened after I left? I wish I could have stayed to see their faces, especially Stanlio and Ollio's."

Francesco laughed and extinguished his cigarette, while Pierre lit another one.

"Well, they weren't incredibly happy."

"What did they do?"

"One of the detectives was shouting to the other: 'What a dickhead, what a dickhead! Why are you standing there like an idiot? Run after him! Go!' So the taller one jumped in a cab and tried to follow you, but came back ten minutes later with the face of a beaten dog, and the other one kept yelling at him: 'Dickhead, dickhead! You let him escape! You lost him!' It was hilarious."

"Good. What about our lovely ladies?"

"Them? Oh, they were just talking to each other about this and that. I had a chat with Gabriella: she seems nice."

"Yeah, she's all right. She's not a troublemaker like the other two."

"Linda and Vanessa told me that they'll be staying until Monday. And guess what: they asked me to let them know if you'd be in touch."

"Oh, you'll do better than that. You'll give them this."

Pierre narrowed his eyes to invisible slits as he let out a cloud of smoke and pushed a sealed envelope across the table.

"What is it?"

"Don't open it now. I want you to read it out loud to them."

"What is it?"

"It's my last will and testament."

"Your—"

"Testament. The grand finale. My first 'posthumous' work." Pierre grinned and took a long drag from his cigarette.

"Look," Francesco continued, "I'd be happy to do it, but the trouble is that I'm leaving today with Chloe."

"You're leaving? Where are you going?"

"Oh, around Europe – perhaps as far as England again. I still have about a week on my InterRail pass."

"Well, a short pause in Rome won't set you back a great deal."

"I'm sorry, Pierre, I don't think—"

"It's the last favour I ask you, then I promise I'll disappear – vanish – whoosh."

Francesco looked at the envelope, then at Pierre's searching eyes, then at the envelope again.

"OK, you've hypnotized me," he said, putting the envelope in his back pocket. "I'll do it. I'll call Vanessa and go and see her this afternoon. She's staying at the Hotel Bernini: it's not far from the station."

"Thank you, sir." Pierre patted him on his forearm. "I knew I could count on you."

"Well, let me pay and get something for Chloe."

"Nah-nah-nah. This one's on me." He ground the cigarette out under his foot and, with a slow, studied movement, put his hand in his pocket and pulled out a fat wad of notes.

"Whoa," Francesco gasped. "Have you robbed a bank?"

"I must admit," Pierre said, counting out fifty thousand lire, "that with money it's so much easier to endure poverty." He gave Francesco an avuncular wink. "Here's the dosh you gave me the other day."

"Cheers."

"And this," Pierre added, producing a 100,000-lire note, "is a present from your friend, a little thank-you for helping him out in a time of penury."

"I don't think I—"

"Keep it." He forced the note into Francesco's hand. "Get the girl a ring. Buy her lunch at the Ritz. You know money burns in my fingers. Take it before it turns into ash."

"All right. Thank you, Pierre." After a pause Francesco added: "What are you going to do now?"

Pierre lit up and inhaled from the last cigarette of his packet before replying.

"Well, I got all my affairs in order: it's all set out in my testament. My demise will be peaceful."

"What shall I do with all those boxes?"

"I'll send instructions from beyond the grave."

"Will I see you again?"

"Maybe you will, maybe you won't. But this is my one parting piece of advice" – he took the longest pull from his cigarette – "do something with your life."

With that he went to the till, paid the bill, waved at Francesco, gave a last wink and rode away down the Corso, leaving a thin trail of smoke behind.

A few minutes later, Francesco was climbing up the steps leading to the old town with a domed tray containing Chloe's cappuccino and *cornetto*, still thinking about Pierre and his final words. As he turned into his street and saw a familiar figure trying to open the door to his flat, Francesco felt his blood tingle in his veins.

"Mum!"

Annamaria looked at him as she pushed the door ajar.

"There you are. There was no answer. Has your friend left?"

"My friend? Oh yes, he's gone. Em, what are you doing here?"

"Picking up your laundry. I couldn't come yesterday. I tried to call you, but—"

"Yes I know," Francesco said, edging inside with a wary step past his mother, "I've been in Rome all day."

Annamaria gave her son a suspicious look, then darted a glance to the tray.

"You treat yourself well in the morning," she said.

"Oh, this? Well, it's Saturday, you know. I like to have my breakfast here, while I read a book and—"

"Can I come in?"

"No no, you stay there, Mum," Francesco shouted, as he cast a quick glance behind his shoulders. "I'll grab the laundry bag and bring it over."

"I have to water the plants."

"The plants are in perfect health – they've never been better in their long vegetal life. You don't wanna drown them with too much water."

But Annamaria was already walking down the corridor and peering in each room to see if everything was in order.

"Mm," was her approving comment when she looked into the main bedroom. "You've made the bed. Was Aunt Teresa here yesterday?"

"I don't know. You sit down in the kitchen while I go and get the dirty clothes, OK?"

"Drink your cappuccino first, or it'll get cold."

"All right."

They sat down at the small kitchen table, and only then – in the light of the window – Francesco noticed that his mother was wearing an elegant dress, lipstick and turquoise eyeshadow, and that her hair was dyed and permed. He didn't remember her looking so good for years.

"Whose wedding is it today?" Francesco asked with a smile.

"Your father's taking me to a restaurant down by the sea."

"Is he? Has he gone mad? Has he won the lottery? What's happened?"

"He got a letter from the German firm that's taking over the steelworks."

"And?" He sipped at his cappuccino.

"And they say they are going to re-employ him. They're offering him a new contract at almost double his previous salary. He's going to be in charge of an entire production department."

"Really? I bet he shaved this morning."

"He did. You should have seen how he was strutting about the house. He's wearing a suit and a tie."

"Wonders will never cease. When is he starting?"

There was a sharp noise from one of the other rooms.

"In September. Was that one of our doors that banged?"

"Must be a draught – an open window." Francesco wiped a trace of perspiration from his upper lip. "So, September. Not a long wait."

"No, and it'll be even shorter: we've decided to go on holiday."

"On holiday? The two of you?"

"For ten days. Venice, Florence and Rome."

Francesco got to his feet and leant over to embrace his mother. "I'm so happy. So happy for you, Mum. And for Dad, too."

"Perhaps good luck is starting to turn our way?"

"Perhaps it is. Perhaps it is, Mum."

Once his mother had gone, Francesco wandered from room to room calling "Chloe! Chloe!", but there was no reply. Where had she gone? Had she managed to sneak out of the flat? He checked in the bathroom, under the bed and even in the cupboard: nothing. She had vanished. Then he had an idea and walked towards the small balcony at the corner of the bedroom. He tried to open the door, but it was locked, and the key was missing.

"Chloe, I know you're hidden out there. You can come back in now."

A few moments later, he heard the key turn in the lock and the door opened.

"You see?" Chloe said with a smile. "When I want, I can make myself weightless, invisible and mute."

"The slamming of the door was a bit of a giveaway."

"It just wouldn't close."

"Come on, let's pack up and leave."

"Where to?"

"The first leg of our journey."

"Give me a kiss. Do you like the way I made the bed?"

"Too middle-class. Perhaps we should rumple it a bit before we go."

16

Rome

THE BERNINI HOTEL has pride of place on one of the most magnificent squares in Rome. With Palazzo Barberini to its left and Via Vittorio Veneto to its right, and overlooking Gian Lorenzo Bernini's Triton Fountain, it offers unashamedly luxurious accommodation to whoever has pockets deep enough to afford it. The wealthy tourist wishing to put things in perspective can also, after a princely breakfast or a sumptuous meal in the hotel, walk only a few yards to the nearby Cappuccini Church and visit its crypts adorned with thousands of human skulls and bones.

Francesco and Chloe arrived at the Bernini in the early afternoon, at a time when the streets of Rome, in August, resemble a sun-scorched desert. Chloe sat in a cool corner of the lobby with her book, Chekhov's *Three Sisters*, while Francesco made his way to the first floor, where Vanessa and the others were waiting for him.

"Hello," Francesco said when he found them, waving his hand. Linda and Vanessa were sitting on a leather sofa, tense expressions on their faces. The two detectives sat opposite them across a low, marble-topped table on which lay two bottles of water and five glasses.

"Gabriella is not here?" Francesco said as he took his place on the damask armchair between the two sofas.

"She's not coming," Vanessa replied with a half-grimace. "She said she had a previous *engagement*. Would you like a drink?"

"Water will be great, thanks."

The taller detective unscrewed the bottle, poured a glass and handed it to him.

"So, what's the story of this new letter?" Linda asked, impatient. "Some new trick?"

"He says it's his 'last will and testament'," Francesco explained, pulling the envelope out of his back pocket.

The balding detective laughed and reached out his hand. "Can I see it?"

Francesco drew the envelope back. "He's asked me to read it out loud to you."

The detective laughed again and shot a long look at the others.

"Come on, we're not going to let him have his way again, I hope?"

The two women looked at each other, then Vanessa said in a frosty tone: "Let's humour him for one last time."

Linda nodded. "Please open it and read it."

Among the stares of the four people around him, Francesco tore across the flap and took out the letter, examining the sheets inside and counting them twice.

"Anything wrong?" the taller detective said.

"It's ten pages front and back, in a very small hand."

"So?"

"I'm just worried I may miss my train this evening."

With no hint of a smile, the balding detective said: "Let's get on with it."

Francesco drank some water, cleared his throat and after a long pause began:

"My dear ladies, this is your late husband speaking to you, as it were, from the Land of Beyond. I know that for one reason or another you'd like to see me six feet under, so you'll be delighted to hear that from now on – as far as you are concerned and to all intents and purposes – I will be dead and buried. However, before I disappear from your lives and set off on that long journey from which no traveller returns, I feel it's my duty to clear up a few things and settle all my earthly affairs. "

Francesco looked up from the pages and saw everyone gazing at him in fierce concentration.

"Before I move on to my will proper," Francesco continued, "I'd like to say a few words in defence of my way of life, and explain how I came to be the man you looked upon as your consort during my passage on earth. My origins are obscure. You know where you are born – some people say – but you don't know where you're going to die. For me the opposite is true. According to what I heard from one of my relatives, I was found on the banks of a river up in Corsica one fine February morning, inside a wicker basket: my mother had decided I should learn how to swim while still a baby, with no lifebelt. Others claim I dropped from the sky after a storm – but they are old folks, and their stories are not to be trusted.

"I have to say that, all in all, things didn't turn out too bad for me. The man who picked me up, whom I came to think of as my father, was a well-known character in that part of the world.

If he *had* been my father, I could have said I had followed in his footsteps. He was a prime stinker, a real good-for-nothing, with four or five families and a whole harem of women. But he was a nice guy, with a heart and three teeth of gold, and I liked him. The only problem was that he wanted me to pursue a career as a thief – and in Corsica thieves aren't all that welcome, especially among the peasants: a bang from a rifle, and that's the end of you. So, when I was twelve, I packed my bags and stowed away on board a ship, and after a week or two they pulled me out by the forelock, more dead than alive. I was taken to a monastery in Liguria, where I was taught my ABCs and my Ave Marias – but I was kept on short rations, so I did a bunk from there too and ended up in the house of a tailor, a widower who was more miserly than three Scottish Shylocks put together. He took a liking to me and decided to adopt me. But I wouldn't even dream of being adopted by him, so I scarpered again, hiding on a train this time, and ended up in Rome."

"Why is he telling us all this bullshit?" the taller detective said. "Can you skip a few pages and get to the main part?"

"He always loved to make a short story long," said Linda.

"If we interrupt him," said Vanessa, "we'll never get to the end of it."

"She's right," the other detective said. "*Continua*."

"Here," Francesco went on, "it wasn't long before a rich lady, a Caritas manager who practised miracle-healing once a week, took me under her wing, cleaned me up and sent me to a good school. A few years later the lady died and left me a neat little sum, and that was when I started to go around the world – Spain, South America, Russia, Greece. Then I got fed up with travelling and remained for longer periods in each country. And as you know, when young men sow their wild oats, it's as if they're sowing wind.

"The first real whirlwind I reaped was when a girl I was going out with told me she had a bun in the oven. I looked her in the eyes and said: 'No no, my dear. You've got a pretty face, but I don't want anyone to build me a coffin so early.' So I left her all my money and moved to another country. There I got into a similar trouble with a young lady I had just promised to marry. You see, despite your every good intention, the first thing women do is look at your feet and think: 'How quickly can I make them sprout with roots?' But that wasn't a game for me. Most people are quite happy to live one life and die one death over the course of fifty, sixty or seventy years. They become lawyers, bankers, businessmen, politicians – they work eighty hours a week and carve out a brilliant career for themselves until they turn into some big shot or big shit. Their wives and kids are safe at home in their suburban mansions – a perfect lawn at the front, a gleaming 4 x 4 parked in the garage and a charming circle of friends to meet up with during the weekend. And what does society do? Society respects these people, admires them, promotes them as models of success – and everyone feels reassured. So long as you keep to your place and fit into the pigeonhole that was created for you, society will let you choose one role and allow you to become whoever you want to be in life. Say you want to work in a hospital, for example, or be a sculptor or a dancer, a singer, a footballer: no problem. But if one life or one career or one family is not enough – if you just try to break out of the chains imposed by our sedentary civilization and live several lives at once – then all hell's let loose: everyone will be after you as if you were the most despicable criminal, the epitome of evil, the scum of the universe."

"What a load of rubbish!" Linda exploded, shaking her red curls.

Vanessa turned to look at her for a moment, then trained her cold eyes back on Francesco.

"Me," he resumed, "I've always been a free agent. I am not content with one job or one career alone. I don't feel satisfied with loving or marrying only one woman. And one destiny is not enough for me: I have the energy, the passion and, above all, the guts to live more than one life. My motto is: live as many lives as you can, because you only have one.

"So you should not point your finger at me simply because I'm different from you and won't live up to your monogamous illusions. We're born free and should remain free throughout our lives, like bees picking up pollen and carrying it from flower to flower."

"He's ranting and rambling," said the taller detective with a smirk.

"Must have been drunk when he wrote this," said the other.

Francesco went on, turning a page.

"Women are greatly overrated, and so are the other two Ws: Work and Wealth. That's what everyone in this world lives for, but there's a lot more to life than that and – call me an idealist if you wish – I believe that the greatest thing we can aspire to is freedom. Not just freedom from the shackles of society, but freedom from ourselves, from the self-imposed cage of inhibitions and restrictions in which we lock up our existence.

"If I had more time, I'd love to talk to you about money and the various delusions associated with it, but I must press on and provide you with a few details about my afterlife.

"First of all, I don't want you to cry for me. I know you won't, but I can assure you that the place where I'm going to park my bones isn't half as bad as the one you're going to inhabit from now on. I will not seek refuge in meditation, but lead an active life. And I won't be embracing celibacy after my bad experience with women: in fact, as you read this, I'll have taken the sacred vows again with my former spouse on the Altar of Heaven."

"What's he on about?" shrieked Linda.

"Sounds like some sort of riddle," said the taller detective, scratching his cheek.

"Complete gibberish," said the other. "Read on."

"And now," Francesco announced, "we come to my last will and testament." There was a silence full of expectation as Francesco paused a few moments for effect. "In his final wishes, Houdini, one of my fellow escapologists, demanded that his wife hold a seance every year so that he could reveal himself. I was tempted to do the same with you, Linda, but I know you are a busy lady, and I doubt you'd want me to turn up even if I were still alive or half-dead. As I said before, my chips have been cashed in, and I won't be walking on the same earth as you any more. Still, I hope I can come back to haunt you one day – either as a bad dream or one of those memories that make your heart sink and your mouth go dry in broad daylight.

"Since you need nothing, I have decided to leave you nothing. I'm so sorry, my dear: the flat in Slotermeer is about to be repossessed, so you'd better start house-hunting. The mortgage payments are over two years in arrears, and banks have been sending me the most harrowing love letters, saying they want to send big, fat, cupid-like bailiffs round. I tried to tell them that their passion is unrequited and no one's there most of the time – I explained you're often engaged in workroom trysts with your *partner*, but there was no point. There's just too much love in this world, and it can't be stopped. Imagine: I saw Christ and Cain playing chess under a tree the other day. That made me almost want to reach out and kiss you goodbye, but I couldn't – and the more I look around in my heart the more I feel I have no other wish other than that you have a barren and empty life."

Linda grinned and shrugged. "He's lying. I've never seen any of the letters he's talking about."

"Maybe he got them redirected to another address?" said the balding detective, casting quick glances around the table.

"Yes. It's possible," said the taller detective, nodding. "But perhaps it's just one of his hoaxes."

"Give me a phone," shouted Linda, jumping to her feet. "Get me a phone right now, please."

"There's nothing you can do on a Saturday afternoon," the balding detective said with an appeasing smile. "You'd better wait until Monday, when you're back in Amsterdam. We'll help you sort everything out, don't worry."

Linda sat down and shook her head in silence.

"Shall I finish reading?" Francesco said, turning the last sheet in his hand. "There's only one page left."

"Go on," said the balding detective, a thin smile still on his lips. "Let that *pagliaccio* entertain us a little longer."

But no one was in the mood for laughter, and Vanessa had the rigid expression of someone braced for a salvo of bad news.

"Let my last thinks all be thanks, as the poet says," Francesco began again. "Without you, Vanessa" – she started when her name was pronounced – "not only the world of sham art but your humble servant Pierre would have been much poorer. Therefore I must thank you for letting me peer into the deep, dark well of your wealth, which I was able in part to redistribute around the world – where I think it belongs – according to my whim and fancy.

"I always knew that your iciness was contagious, but I was amazed to see how quickly you managed to freeze my offshore bank accounts. Now, it looks like Christmas has come early for you too, and you'll be in for a long winter. You'll soon receive a letter from a museum in Israel, thanking you for donating dozens of your paintings, as well as some of the most precious works from the Schreiber Trust's collection. Don't be rude or too cold, and send them a gracious acknowledgement, will you? After all, this goes only a short way to giving back what was taken away from them unlawfully."

Francesco looked at Vanessa for a moment: she kept blinking in silence and maintained an expressionless mask.

"Furthermore," he continued, "if you don't want to see your picture on the front page of every newspaper in Germany from *Die Welt* to the *Pforzheimer Zeitung*, I suggest you let me have access again to my hard-earned savings and bolster them with a voluntary contribution from your gold-bullion reserves. Make sure this is commensurate to my previous lifestyle, as life after death can be fairly expensive.

"My last wish is that you give up painting altogether. Trust a connoisseur and a lover of beauty: it doesn't cut it. Your art lacks passion, it lacks a soul: it doesn't feel like you're having fun when you do it. You should consider moving to warmer climates – that may help you thaw your life a bit. Adieu."

"Is that all?" said the taller detective.

"That's all," said Francesco.

"What an idiot."

"I've got it," exclaimed Vanessa, straightening her back. "I think I've got it."

"What?" the detectives blurted out.

"The riddle."

"The what?"

"He said he's taken his vows again on the Altar of Heaven with his former wife. It means he's getting married again in the Aracoeli church – St Mary of the Altar of Heaven – with Gabriella. This is why she didn't come and she isn't mentioned in his 'will'."

The two detectives exchanged a puzzled look.

"Ara—"

"Saint—"

They glanced at the two women, then looked at each other again.

"Let's make a move," said the balding detective, getting to his feet. "Perhaps we can still catch him, if we're quick."

Francesco cleared his throat. "I don't think I'm coming," he said.

They all stopped to look at him.

"I've got a train to catch later on," he added.

Vanessa leant over and gave him two hurried kisses on his cheeks.

"Thank you. Thank you for everything," she said.

The taller detective produced a business card and handed it to him.

"If he gets in touch, give us a ring. There'll be a big reward."

"Sure."

He saw the two sleuths rush down the stairs towards the main entrance, followed gingerly by the two women in high heels, then made his way to the lobby, where Chloe was still immersed in her book.

"Are you finished?" she asked.

"I hope so. I'll tell you everything later. Let's go."

Outside, the sun was beating its unmitigated glare on the asphalt. Chloe and Francesco were walking up Via Barberini, back towards Stazione Termini, when they were confronted with an amusing scene on the other side of the road. The taller detective was walking round his silver Alfetta bent double like an oversized monkey, shrieking: "He's slashed our tyres again! All of them! All of them!", while the two women stood transfixed on the pavement and the other detective tried to spot an improbable taxi and shouted: "What a dickhead! What a dickhead!"

They walked on and left them there in that pickle, and were crossing the little square in front of the Fontana dell'Acqua Felice when a gentle honk attracted their attention. It came from a red Duetto parked in the shade on the far corner of the square. A hand holding a cigarette stuck out and made a lazy waving motion, and a corsair grin flashed at them.

"Pierre!" Francesco called. Gabriella was sitting in the passenger seat. He and Chloe went over and greeted the couple. "Good to see you're still alive."

Pierre chuckled, then took a drag from his cigarette. "So, how did my last will and testament go down?"

"Not too bad, not too bad. The two guys didn't seem very happy with what you did to their car, though."

"Heh heh heh. They'll learn not to provoke me next time. They'll need wings if they want to catch me – wings. Where are they now?"

"Probably on their way to the Altar of Heaven."

"Heh heh. But it's too late for them now, too late. We're already on honeymoon, aren't we dear?" Gabriella looked at him from under her sunglasses and gave a wan smile. "I wish I could watch them running up those hundred-odd steps to the top under this dog-day heat, but we have better things to do." He flicked the cigarette butt away. "Would you like a lift to Termini?"

Francesco shook his head. "I don't think we'd be comfortable sitting on the bonnet."

Pierre looked behind his shoulder and laughed. "I forgot I'm driving this sardine can now. Well, so long then."

"So long, Pierre." They shook hands. "Have you decided what to do with those boxes?"

"Oh, don't worry, I'll be in touch. I'll be in touch soon."

He turned the ignition on, waved his hand again, and the car roared away across the cobbles of the piazza, leaving burnt rubber, until it disappeared down Via XX Settembre, to the accompaniment of several more honkings of the horn.

Chloe and Francesco remained rooted to the ground for a few moments, looking into one another's eyes with an expression that was half questioning and half amused. Then, hand in hand and with a broad smile on their young faces, they continued in silence towards Piazza della Repubblica.

It crossed Francesco's mind that they also had better things to do.

EPILOGUE

Many journeys later

Twenty years are a long, daunting stretch in the brief lifespan of a man. So many roads are taken, so many crossroads are traversed during that time. And at every step a new turning, with every action a new cause-and-effect connection in the unfathomable chain of events: the flutter of a butterfly's wings causing a huge storm somewhere else in the world.

Francesco had recently turned forty-one, and one evening he had to go out but could not find his car keys. Frustrated, he went into his bedroom and started rummaging in the bedside cabinet's drawer. There, thrown together over a number of years, was a jumble of disparate objects, including three belts, two old leather wallets, earplugs, a chequebook, a black tie, unused cuff links, a sleeping mask, a medal for running a half-marathon, a mobile-phone adaptor, two small locks with their keys, an expired passport, his first *London Streetfinder*, a wooden clothes peg, a block of orange Post-its, a book catalogue, a yellow packet with his eldest daughter's first lost tooth, a three-year-old box of Durex, buttons, coins, pens, tube caps, train tickets, loyalty cards, business cards of forgotten people, credit-card receipts and party invitations.

Francesco sighed. "What a mess."

He looked at his watch and shook his head, then he spotted a plastic wallet with the words "*INTER RAIL*" in dark blue resting against the back of the drawer. He picked it up and pulled out the folded booklet and the train tickets inside. On the front he saw his name, his date of birth, his signature, the travel card's cost in the now defunct lire: 390,000 – which still seemed quite cheap for an entire month of freedom and adventure. He opened the booklet and leafed through the various stops on his journey twenty years ago: Bologna, München, Köln, Berlin, Wittenberg – all with their dates and the stamps from the ticket collectors. It all came back to him in a flood of memories: the places he had visited, the things he had done, the people he had met during his trip across Europe – Vanessa's parcel, the accident in Amsterdam, the scrapes in London, the win in Monte Carlo, Pierre.

A voice called him.

"One moment," he shouted. "I'm coming."

He began to wonder what would have happened if by any chance he had taken the train to Prague rather than the one to Lund that night in Berlin, who would be calling him from the other room if he had not missed his appointment with Elke, in which country and city would he be living if Christer had not come back to his flat that evening or if Kyle had turned up that Saturday in London. Would he be a teacher now? Or an actor, a lawyer, a businessman? Would he see a neatly mowed lawn and a large family car outside his window? Would he have any kids? Which language would they speak? What would be their names?

Tucked among the tickets to the Italian border and the fast-train upgrades he found Pierre's "testament". He read it again after many years and could not help smiling at his old friend's words. God only knew what had happened to him. He'd said he'd be in touch, but had in fact vanished altogether. His boxes of books were still hidden away in Grandma Lina's cupboard, and no other title by Lele Fante seemed to have come out in Italy. If he was still alive, he must be around sixty now. Perhaps he had settled down somewhere, perhaps he had continued his nomadic existence and still moved from country to country, woman to woman and life to life, changing identities, breaking hearts, stealing fortunes. Perhaps he was publishing works under a different name, perhaps he was yachting with Mr Glinskis. At times, when Francesco heard the sound of a whistle or a honk, he half-expected to see Pierre waving or winking at him, cigarette in hand, from the seat of some flashy sports car. What would Pierre think of him? What would he say? Had Francesco "done something" with his life? He had a lovely house, a caring wife, two gorgeous kids, a successful job and a comfortable income. Could he have done more? Lived more lives than just the one that had built itself around him? Is it better to try and force your way onto different paths or enjoy your destiny and surrender to it?

Three years after his last meeting with Pierre, as he was reading the "Strange but True" section in a crossword magazine, Francesco had come across the following short article:

The American Ray Duncan, a former male model, forty-three years old, was married to four different women at once, and succeeded in keeping these marriages going in such a way that each wife continued to be unaware of the existence of the others. When his crime was discovered and he was arrested by the police last December, he declared that, although he faced up to five years in jail, he was happy his life was about to change: the effort of having to conceal the facts, and the exertion involved in keeping four wives on the go, had made his life "one long hell".

For a few moments Francesco had wondered whether this wasn't another of Pierre's assumed identities, but Ray Duncan's nationality and his former career as a model were at odds with the background of his old friend.

In more recent times, Francesco had read articles on the life and misdeeds of Christophe Rocancourt – impersonator, con artist and playboy – who for many years, with his lies and elegant manners, had taken in everyone in New York high society. But even in that case, despite the strange resemblance of several details – such as the languages he spoke (Italian, French and English), the rumours about his relationship with the Rockefeller family, and the fact that Rocancourt too claimed to be an orphan, there were too many aspects that didn't fit the bill, in particular his age. All the same, it was surprising to discover that there were other people who followed the dictates of Pierre's unorthodox philosophy of life – with the sole difference that these men had been arrested while Pierre seemed to have got away with it.

Of all the people who had crowded Francesco's month of travels, Pierre was not the only one to have gone out of his life. Francesco had had no further contact with Kyle or Elke, and had no idea whether their destinies had taken them to happiness, tragedy or a boring middle age. As for Vanessa, according to the various references he was able to find on the web, in the late '90s she had married the CEO of a multinational in the petrochemical sector. Her work was still exhibited in the most important galleries and museums in the world, but she seemed to have abandoned painting and turned her hand instead to a form of "transcendental" and "metaphysical" sculpture. There was no reference to Pierre on her Wikipedia page or in any of her other online biographies, as if he had never existed. There was no mention, either, of her father and grandfather, of her revolutionary pamphlet or of any scandal or controversy about her family origins. Just page after page of praise and reviews of her works. A few months ago, there had been a big retrospective of her art in Venice, and Francesco was tempted to go and see if the little furrow had vanished from her brow, and if she was still as beautiful as he remembered her to be – but in the end he decided not to make the trip. Instead, he bought one of her smaller "Oneiric" paintings from an Internet dealer and hung it in his studio.

For some time Francesco had managed to stay in touch with Boudewyn in Amsterdam, until his friend had moved to the Dutch countryside after marrying a Ukrainian girl. A letter he got from him in 2002 cast a spooky light on the mysterious events in the Slotermeer apartment block ten years before. Boudewyn informed him that a similar accident had taken place in the building a few months after he had moved out of his flat. The victim, a twenty-year-old student from Rotterdam who had been visiting a friend, was found with a broken skull in a pool of blood on the third floor. The student survived the attack, but could not remember who or what had hit him. A thorough investigation was conducted by the police, but none of the residents – nor Mephisto, who had moved back to Ireland in the meantime – appeared to be implicated. Many things in life are bound to remain unresolved, and Francesco had to accept that this was one of them.

The only friendship that had remained alive across the years was the one with Leonardo. Undeterred by the absence of any reply from Lele Fante to his numerous letters, Leo had finally managed to become a distinguished author. At least that's how he thought of himself after winning, together with another nineteen budding writers, an open competition organized by the Ugo Papetti Research Centre in Monticchio, and after having two of his stories accepted by Mayfly, a digital publisher "specializing in works of an ephemeral and transitory nature". Every few months Francesco received some of Leo's poetry via email, which his friend was trying to place for publication abroad, since the Italian market had become totally *emasculated*.

That day in August twenty years ago, Francesco was not only leaving for a new journey. The final words of Rilke's sonnet – *"Du musst dein Leben ändern"* – were ringing in his ears when he took that evening train with Chloe. He had decided to break away from his current existence and move on to a fresh life. He used the money from his Monte Carlo win to buy some clothes and a suitcase for his travels, and pay a deposit on a new place to live. When, a week later, he phoned his parents from London, it was his father who answered.

"You don't think it's time for you to come back?" Sergio had said.

"I'm not coming back, Dad."

"You're not coming back?"

"I'm staying here in England."

There was a very long pause.

"Do what you like. So long as you don't come knocking on my door for money one day. You know what I think, son: when the ant decides to die—" And Sergio hung up.

Walking out of Victoria Station with Chloe, Francesco felt as if he was emerging from his chrysalis: in front of him lay the big wide world and an unconstrained life of infinite possibilities.

He heard quick steps advancing down the corridor, and saw a little hand open the bedroom door.

"Daddy," said Arabella, his youngest, with a wide smile from under her curly blond hair, "Mummy's found the keys."

"Mm?"

"Come, come with me. I'll show you where they are."

Francesco put the InterRail wallet back where he had found it and closed the drawer, then got to his feet and reached to take his daughter's hand.

Together, they went into the living room. Chloe was sitting on the sofa winding a ball from loops of wool that Laura, their eldest, was holding in front of her with outstretched arms.

"There," Arabella said, pointing at the mantelpiece. "Behind the clock."

"Ah." Francesco sighed. "The cleaners. I could have looked for hours."

"What were you doing in the bedroom?"

He turned to look at Chloe's smiling, beautiful face.

"Oh, travelling back in time."

"Well," Chloe said in a mock-reproachful tone, finishing the ball and getting up, "you should teach me too, because we're twenty minutes late."

"Twenty minutes late?" he said, almost startled. *I think we're twenty years late*, he wanted to add. *Why don't we leave everything, jump on a train and...*

Instead, he put the keys in his pockets and, once Chloe and the girls had stepped out, switched off the lights in the hall, casting a quick look around the dark house before closing the door behind him.

ACKNOWLEDGEMENTS

I would like to thank Andrew Brown, who translated an early version of the book I had written in Italian: many of his jokes and inventive turns of phrase have been preserved in this final version. Many thanks to my brother Mirco for his support and his observations on various drafts of the novel. I am grateful to Ian Thomson for letting me use the story of the mysterious attack in the Amsterdam chapter. A big thank you goes to Tim Bates of Pollinger Ltd, who encouraged me to go back to my original idea of the novel, and all the friends and editors – in particular Mike Stocks and Alexander Middleton – who have helped me to improve it.